KISS AND TELL

BETH BOLDEN

CHAPTER ONE

NOT ONLY WAS JACKSON Finley's brain tired, his eyes were fuzzy, the figures blurring together on the screen. Even worse, his stomach had reached a point beyond merely growling. If he didn't eat soon, the pathetic succulent on the edge of his desk—barely hanging on to life—might start to look appetizing. Considering his brother had given him the plant in an attempt to win the argument that "you can't even keep a succulent alive," eating it might not be the best idea Jackson had ever had.

Those three pieces of evidence taken, either separately or together, should have been enough to tell him it was long past time for him to shut his laptop.

He leaned back in his chair, knowing he should, but still wanting to get through the reconciliation of the last three days of sales. Jackson squinted, and realized he could barely see the clock in the bottom right-hand corner of his screen. It couldn't be after ten, could it?

His stomach growled again, even louder this time.

Jackson guessed it could.

He'd been here since before ten this morning, which meant he'd been at the Funky Cup, the bar he owned with his brother, for over twelve hours.

Sadly, not even the longest shift he'd pulled this month . . . *not even the longest shift this week,* Jackson mentally corrected.

He tried to refocus back to the numbers swimming in front of his eyes, but they just wouldn't stay solid *or* still.

Just when he was about to call it quits and give up, his office door opened.

There was only one person who would ever just walk in without knocking: his brother, Shaw.

Sure enough, Jackson heard Shaw's boots thumping on the floorboards and he looked up to see his brother, a concerned look on his face.

"I thought," Shaw said without a greeting, "that there was no way you were still in here working and you must've slipped away without me noticing, but nope, here you are. Still."

"It's been a long day," Jackson agreed.

An understatement.

His stomach rumbled again, loudly enough that Shaw must've been able to hear it, because he did a double take. "Excuse me," his brother said. "Was that your *stomach?*"

"I might have missed dinner," Jackson said testily.

"You mean you *skipped* dinner again," Shaw said. "The kitchen would be happy to bring you anything you wanted, you know that." He threw his hands up. "I don't know why I bother trying to reason with you, when you're so fucking unreasonable."

"I had a lot to do," Jackson said.

"Yeah, and you've got one more thing to do," Shaw said. "Get your ass outside. There's a new food truck parked there, and I want you to get something to eat."

"Another one?" Jackson said, prying his ass out of his chair. He stretched again, his back cracking. "I think you're collecting these guys."

"This one's from Portland," Shaw said, following him out of his office. "And he sells the best goddamn hummus I've ever had in my life."

"Hummus?" Jackson said dubiously.

"You think you've had hummus before, but you're going to realize that you were just preparing for the day you were lucky enough to try *real* hummus," Shaw said.

Jackson rolled his eyes. "You are ridiculous. Get *your* ass back to the bar."

Shaw gave him a quasi-salute, grinning the whole time. "Yes, sir, yes, boss."

Jackson swatted him on the shoulder. "I am *not* your boss. Well, technically yes, but . . ."

It was complicated. Yes, Jackson owned the Funky Cup—at least fifty-one percent of it. Forty-nine percent of it belonged to Shaw. He could thank their father for that particularly bizarre division of assets. He'd always wanted the bar to go to his two sons, but he'd said in his will that he knew one of them would need to be "in charge" or they'd end up killing each other.

Some days Jackson wasn't sure that wasn't going to happen anyway, but he appreciated that his dad had known his sons well enough to realize that they wouldn't always agree.

"Enough of my boss to tell me to get my ass behind the bar," Shaw retorted.

"People look thirsty," Jackson pointed out before he pushed the front door open, and took a long, deep gulp of fresh air. Well, as fresh as the air was in Los Angeles, anyway.

The truck that Shaw had mentioned was parked next to the Funky Cup's entrance. The bar had a kitchen, but it closed around nine, and since the Funky Cup was often open till two in the morning, Shaw had taken to making informal arrangements with some of his food truck buddies. One or two of them would park next to the bar for a few hours after the kitchen closed.

Tonight, there was just the one.

"The Big Fat Greek Truck," Jackson said under his breath, reading the colorful blue and white flag painted on the side of the shiny silver truck.

He looked over at the menu, taped to one side of the plexiglass window, and his stomach growled again, sounding like an angry bear attempting to escape, Alien-style. Every item he read sounded better than the last.

"Hey."

Jackson looked over, and there was a young guy, maybe in his late twenties, with dark hair and striking dark eyes, leaning down so he could meet Jackson's eyes through the window.

"Hey," he responded.

"You hungry?" the guy asked. "'Cause I got food." He broke into a bright grin, infectious and winning, and Jackson felt it down deep, somewhere he had no business feeling smiles. Especially smiles from strangers.

Shaw had befriended this food truck owner, so the chances were high he was queer, but that didn't mean that he was available or interested. Maybe he was just trying to sell some hummus and a gyro.

"I'm starving, actually," Jackson said.

"You look it," the guy said, somewhat critically. "Tired and hungry."

Jackson rolled his eyes. Just in case his ego needed a check, here was this guy who reminded him that his best guy-catching years were almost definitely behind him. A lot of his old party friends had assumed that because he now *owned* the bar, he enjoyed more hookups than ever, but the truth was, he worked way too hard to have the energy. He couldn't even remember the last time he'd gone home with someone.

Maybe he *was* old. Old and tired.

And starving.

"Then you should feed me," Jackson said shortly.

"You got it," the guy said, and disappeared before even taking his order. Jackson nearly pounded on the window. Apparently it wasn't enough that the stranger had told him he looked tired, but now, instead of feeding him, he'd gone MIA.

"My fucking life," Jackson muttered to himself, and was just about to turn to go when he heard a sound, and followed by a cheery, "I've got you."

Jackson looked up and there was a tray in the window, loaded with food. "What's this?" he asked.

The guy shot him another one of those lopsided, charming smiles. "Your dinner, what else?" he said.

Reaching up, Jackson took the tray before the guy could disappear again, and this time with the food. "What do I owe you?" he asked.

Maybe it was a little weird that he hadn't asked Jackson what he wanted to order, but then, this was one of his brother's friends. They were all a little odd, and besides, Jackson wasn't going to look a gift horse in the mouth, because everything on the tray looked delicious and smelled even better.

"Nothing," the guy said, shaking his head. "It's on the house."

"What?" Jackson, who'd been reaching for his wallet, glanced up in surprise. "No, seriously, let me pay for it."

"All the payment I need is to see you fed," the guy said. "Next time."

Jackson was going to say there probably wasn't going to be a next time, but the owner shot him another grin and an, "Eat up!" and then disappeared out of sight again.

"Seriously," Jackson muttered. He took the tray and, instead of going back inside, skirted around the corner of the bar and, using the code on the side door lock, let himself into the back patio. It was still pretty early for food service workers, their main clientele, so even though Shaw had set the fire pit going, the area was mostly empty. Jackson grabbed a picnic table, set his food on it, and sat down.

Jackson had just scooped up some hummus with a perfectly soft yet crisp-edged piece of pita bread when a voice interrupted him.

"Late dinner?"

Tony Blake, one of Shaw's food truck owner friends, slid into the seat opposite Jackson's.

Jackson ignored him, and shoved the pita bread into his mouth in one big bite, and then immediately wished he hadn't. Shaw was often right about food—Jackson often let him deal with the head of the kitchen when it came to the menu, and he had all these friends who owned food trucks—but he'd been *really* right this time around. This hummus was . . . ethereally light and smooth on the tongue, but packed a nearly indescribable flavor punch. Lemon, garlic, the smooth unctuousness of really good olive oil, even a tiny bite of spice at the end—it had it all.

Everything that Jackson had never wondered hummus could be, and that this hummus did without even trying.

"Let me guess," Tony continued speaking, not letting Jackson commune in perfect, reverent silence with his new favorite food on earth, "you've just tried Alexis' hummus for the first time."

Jackson chewed and swallowed a second bite. Somehow, impossibly, it was even better than the first had been. He scooped up a third. "His name is Alexis?" Jackson didn't know why it mattered, but it did.

Nodding, Tony snuck one of the *dolmas*, stuffed grape leaves, off Jackson's plate. "Hey," Jackson said, smacking Tony's arm. "Yes, this is my dinner. And according to both Shaw and apparently Alexis, I'm going to waste away into nothing if I don't eat. If you keep stealing, I will tell on you."

Tony grinned. "You *do* look a little worn out."

"Not you too," Jackson said. "You guys keep acting like I'm at death's door. I'm fine, just . . ."

"A little overworked?" Tony said after taking a drink of his beer.

"There's a lot of work to be done," Jackson said defensively.

"And you wouldn't be you if you didn't try to take all of it on yourself," Tony pointed out.

"Exactly." Jackson examined the rest of the plate and, deciding on a *dolmas*, because there was a strong possibility Tony *might* eat them all, popped it into his mouth. He expected the explosion of flavor this time—garlic and lemon and something earthier, richer—but it still took his breath away.

"Eggplant," Tony said, and Jackson did a double take. "I spent an hour talking to the guy, trying to convince him to tell me what it was, and he finally admitted that it was roasted eggplant."

Jackson ate another *dolmas,* and yeah, he could tell. Definitely eggplant. "Maybe he wouldn't be very happy that you're gossiping about his secret ingredients," he said primly. Even though he should absolutely not care—or *think*—about Alexis.

He was undeniably cute, and he was an incredible cook, but even if Alexis liked men and was amenable to hooking up, Jackson didn't have the time. He knew that. But his mind persisted in wondering, anyway.

"It's not really a secret, I think he just wanted to make me guess," Tony mumbled, suddenly very interested in the way the label on his bottle of beer was peeling off.

"Oh, I like him already," Jackson retorted. Of all Shaw's friends, Tony Blake was the most infuriating and also the most charming. Jackson liked him despite never intending to. He'd been coming to the bar since he moved to Los Angeles a few years back, and honestly, if Jackson had ever thought about it, he probably would have counted Tony as one of *his* friends too.

"What?" Tony yelped.

"Anyone who makes you work harder than you want to, I'm officially a fan of. That's why I like Lucas so much," Jackson said, referring to Tony's boyfriend. "I have it on good authority that he *definitely* makes you work hard."

"Every single day," Tony said without an ounce of shame.

Another reason that Jackson had always liked the guy.

"You should try the chicken gyro," Tony suggested when Jackson started poking around the rest of the plate. "The things that man does to chicken . . . I didn't think they were possible."

Jackson picked up the gyro and nearly moaned when he bit into it. Tony was annoyingly right. The chicken was flawlessly seasoned as well as being unbelievably tender and juicy. Alexis had stuffed it in one of those soft, chewy, crispy-edged pitas, tucked alongside a bunch of fresh veggies and the most divine tzatziki Jackson had ever had. And Jackson had eaten a *lot* of Greek food over the years.

"So," Jackson said, setting down his pita, "if this guy Alexis is so obviously great, why isn't he going to be part of your food truck lot?" Shaw had told him the list the other night and he hadn't remembered Shaw mentioning any newbies.

"Believe me," Tony said fervently, "I wish I could convince him to stick around. But he's from Portland originally, and really just passing through, before he heads to Austin."

"He's going to Texas?" Anyone who *chose* to go to Texas was always baffling to Jackson, who'd gotten out and had never looked back.

"Yeah. He's got a solid lead on a really popular food truck community there. They want him, *bad*."

Jackson was thinking that anyone would. Had they seen the guy? Had they eaten his food? It was not exactly a difficult conclusion to come to.

"You should convince him to stay," Jackson said. "You could persuade water to be dry."

"I've been trying," Tony said with a shrug. "So far, no dice. But maybe . . ." His eyes gleamed in the dim light. "Maybe *you* should give it a try."

"What?" Jackson squawked. "Me? Why?"

"He's single, you're single. You've been single forever, to hear Shaw tell it."

"You shouldn't be listening to Shaw," Jackson said firmly. God, it was embarrassing enough that he hadn't been with anyone in forever—he didn't need his freaking brother telling everyone about how pathetic he was.

"Yeah, but you didn't deny it," Tony teased. "Seriously though, talk to the guy. Maybe you'll like him."

"He's moving to Texas, and Texas is the very last place I would ever voluntarily go," Jackson said.

"Exactly," Tony pointed out. "You can convince him to stay here, with us."

"You're crazy," Jackson said, shaking his head. "If anyone can convince him, it's you. Not me."

Tony drained the rest of his beer and stood. "Finish your dinner and just . . . think about it, okay?"

Jackson rolled his eyes, because of course he wasn't going to think about it. The very idea was ludicrous.

But he still said, "Okay."

Chapter Two

And, despite all Jackson's better intentions, he was still thinking about it a week later.

At first, he'd told himself it was only because Tony was so obnoxious and so good at getting under everyone's skin. That was all. He hadn't really been serious, and he hadn't really meant it, anyway. The suggestion that he persuade Alexis to stay was just Tony being Tony.

Then he'd convinced himself he was only thinking about it still because of the food.

His brother had caught him twice checking out, as unobtrusively as possible, the handwritten food truck schedule that Shaw had taped behind the bar. "Hey," he'd tried to say as casually as possible, "when's that Greek food truck coming back?"

He'd actually *worried* that the guy had already gone to Texas. That should've been the first indication, but Jackson was good at pretending things were different than they really were. Take his work schedule, for example.

But Shaw had only shrugged and said, "Oh, he's been in high demand and it's just him, you know. 'Cause he likes to travel light."

It was even crazier that the guy made all that delicious food by himself.

Jackson had nodded, like he understood completely, even as he internally, irrationally wailed that life was not fair and he wanted some of that hummus *now*. And if he happened to see Alexis again, with his dark hair and even darker eyes and bewitchingly mysterious smile, that would just be an added bonus. That was all.

The third reason actually lay with Shaw.

"I think you need to stop working so much, hiding away in that office," Shaw had said three days after they'd had the conversation about Alexis and why he hadn't been back at the curb outside the Funky Cup. "We include me on the regular staff schedule every week. Why aren't you on there?"

"Because I'm the owner. My hours are . . . flexible." Jackson had ducked his head out for a few minutes, to clear his head and since it was a Wednesday night and still early, it was slow and Shaw had nothing better to do than to corner him on his favorite conversational topic—Jackson's work habits.

"We can afford to hire a bookkeeper, you know," Shaw said.

Jackson rolled his eyes. "How do you know what we can afford to hire?"

"I read the reports you send," Shaw claimed.

"No, you don't," Jackson said. He knew his brother. Too well, probably. Reports of any kind made Shaw's eyes glaze over. His strengths weren't numbers and columns and profit and loss. His real talent lay with people. He was like Tony in that he could charm anyone, and in addition, could get anyone to open up, to make them feel better by mixing the right drink, by saying the right words at exactly the right time.

In other words, he was an ideal bartender.

But an accountant? Not his strong suit.

Jackson didn't even think of himself as particularly adept financially—which was why he worked so hard at it. Their father had left them the Funky Cup, and he had zero intention of frittering away the family legacy with poor management.

"Actually, I did, last night," Shaw said. "It was horribly slow, and you were *still* in that goddamned office, so I pulled them out."

"And fell asleep at the bar?" Jackson retorted.

"No. They were actually interesting reading. We're . . ." Shaw dropped his voice. "We're actually doing really well?"

"Don't sound so surprised," Jackson said. "I don't work this hard for nothing."

"No, you don't, and I don't say it enough, so I'll say it now: I appreciate everything you've done. You took a lot of this on when you really didn't want to, and when I was completely unsuited for it, and I appreciate it." Shaw shot him a reproving look. "But you're losing yourself in this place and it's not a loss I'm going to take sitting down. And you shouldn't either."

The words hit Jackson harder than he'd anticipated they would. Probably harder than Shaw had anticipated they would; except no, Jackson could see the hard look in Shaw's eyes. The tough love emanating from his open expression. He absolutely wanted his words to sit badly with Jackson. To fester. To build.

"All I'm saying is that we can afford to hire some help for you. And we *should*."

"I'll think about it," Jackson said brusquely, because he knew he wouldn't be able to do anything else. If this week was any sign, all his stray, irritating thoughts weren't ever going to stay locked away in their individual boxes.

It was a curse—and maybe a little bit of a blessing.

"And," Shaw added, gaze hardening even further, "I want you to promise to come to the New Year's Eve party."

"What?" Jackson practically screeched.

"It used to be one of your favorite holidays, and you haven't even come to the party the last few years."

"I've been at the bar every single one of those years," Jackson protested.

"In your *office*. On *New Year's Eve*."

Shaw's words were damning. "Yeah, I guess I was," Jackson admitted.

"It's fucking ridiculous. You can take one night off, and frankly, you could fucking use it. Find some cute guy to kiss. Maybe even get laid. Let go and let loose. Once a year won't kill you *or* the bar."

Shaw's words rang with way more truth than Jackson was comfortable confronting.

He had become a workaholic, if he couldn't even take one night off a year. And Shaw was right, he'd used to love New Year's Eve. Had indulged in way too many ill-advised but undoubtedly fun kisses and hookups. Had gotten drunk. Had partied like the night was the dawn of a new age, instead of just a new year.

"I'll think about that too," Jackson said.

"No," Shaw said steadily. "You're coming, if I have to drag you out of that office myself."

"Okay, okay, geez," Jackson said, even though he was secretly a little bit pleased. Shaw was very laid-back and often let most things go, but he seemed to be a dog with a bone on this subject. They didn't talk much about brotherly love or affection, but it was hard to see Shaw's insistence as anything else.

"You'll be here, and not in your office," Shaw said, a smile beginning to creep onto his face.

"I'll be here, and *not* in the office," Jackson agreed.

Three days later, Jackson was regretting his promise.

Not because he was really wanting to lock himself away with work for the evening, but because he wasn't sure he knew how to do this anymore.

After helping Shaw oversee the final party arrangements, he'd gone home to shower and change for the big night. Shaw lived in the rooms above the bar, but a few years back, Jackson had bought a little cottage that he'd intended to remodel. Well, remodeling required time and energy, none of which Jackson seemed to have left after his work for the day.

"Maybe Shaw has a point," Jackson said, staring in the moisture-fogged mirror pensively. The bathroom tile was clean, because he made sure his house was clean, if barely used, but it was old and cracked and frankly, *ugly*.

It had never bothered him before now, because he was usually too tired or preoccupied to think about it. But he remembered now, that when he'd bought the house, he'd made all kinds of promises to himself about updating it and making it *his*. And they'd all fallen by the wayside as the bar had continued to prosper.

Having the money in the bank should've made it easier, but he'd taken his dad's words, written in his will, to heart. It was *his* responsibility to make sure the bar stayed afloat and took care of not only himself, but his brother, too. So he hadn't wanted to touch the savings that he meticulously added to every month. But the truth was, there was plenty of money for him to remodel his house. Plenty of money if Shaw wanted to buy instead of continuing to live over the bar. But they'd both gotten fairly stuck in their own ruts—that much was becoming painfully obvious.

"You're going to do something about yours," Jackson said to the mirror. "Tonight, you are going to find a cute guy and at least flirt with him a little. It's been way too long."

Jackson recognized the problem with that particular plan when he opened his closet, only to be confronted by mostly t-shirts and jeans. There'd been a time when he'd really loved experimenting with fashion—he hadn't been a clotheshorse necessarily, but he'd gotten close to it. Did any of those clothes still fit him? Did he even have them still?

Digging deep into his closet, he pulled out a worn jean jacket that he used to *love*, that he swore he hadn't worn since before he'd inherited the bar. He paired that with his favorite pair of dark-wash jeans, and a plain black t-shirt, fixed his hair, and decided, staring in the mirror, that however he looked was going to have to be good enough for that mythical cute guy he was going to flirt with.

When he got to the Funky Cup, Shaw was already busy behind the bar, alongside the other bartenders. Everyone was working tonight, including him . . . *sort of.*

He'd just leaned over a spot of empty bar, hoping to catch Shaw's eye and grab a beer, when Jackson heard a voice behind him.

"How was the food?" The voice was low, intimate, and gruff around the edges. It was an undeniably sexy voice, and for that reason alone, Jackson was sure that the question wasn't meant for him, but for one of the other guys milling around the bar area.

Technically, the Funky Cup was not a gay bar, but especially on nights like these, when they closed for a private party, it definitely became more a gay bar than anything else because of all Shaw's friends.

A finger tapped on his shoulder. Jackson turned, and his breath caught in his chest. It was the guy from the Greek food truck, and he was smiling at Jackson, like he'd just won the lottery.

"How was the food?" he asked again. "You look . . ." The guy (*Alexis,* Jackson mentally corrected, Tony told you his name is *Alexis*) grinned. "Much better. Not quite as hungry."

"I don't know," Jackson said, "I could eat something." *You, alive.* "And you know the food was incredible. Best Greek food I've ever eaten. Best hummus. That stuff is addictive, like crack."

"I've heard that before," Alexis said, coming up to stand next to Jackson at the bar. "But it means something, coming from a guy like you."

"A guy like me?" Jackson raised an eyebrow.

Alexis had the nerve to blush a little. Jackson was fairly certain that his pulse wasn't as steady as it normally was. "You're close to Shaw, right?" he said. "Shaw knows his shit. Therefore," he added, "you must too."

So, Alexis did not know he was Shaw's brother and the owner of the bar. Jackson hesitated, wondering if he should tell him the truth.

"I'm Alexis, by the way," he said, "and you're?"

"The man of your dreams," Jackson teased.

Alexis rolled his eyes, which only made Jackson like him more. "What do you know about my dreams?"

"Not as much as I'd like to," Jackson admitted. "But for what it's worth, I'm Jackson, Jackson Finley."

Alexis' eyes widened. "You're Shaw's brother."

Jackson nodded. "And I own this bar." He was afraid it was going to scare Alexis off, before he got more than a few flirtatious comments in, but he wanted to tell the truth. Because now that he knew Alexis was here, he wanted more than just a few minutes of flirting with a cute guy. He wanted a kiss at midnight.

And he wanted it with Alexis.

"Hey, you two." Out of the corner of his eye, Jackson saw Shaw approach. "What can I get you?"

"Vodka," Alexis said. "Neat."

Before Alexis' order, Jackson had intended to get a beer. Yes, he was at the party, and he was not technically working, but he also had intended to keep his wits about him, just in case he needed to be available for some kind of emergency. But from the look Shaw was giving him, it was clear the bar was going to have to burn to the ground before his brother got him involved in anything work-related.

"Make that two," Jackson said.

"You want something good, I assume," Shaw said, pulling out two squat glasses, and a long, tall frosted bottle. "None of that flavored shit."

Alexis' nose crinkled adorably. "Uh, *no*," he said. "Anyone who flavors vodka is committing an abomination."

"Aren't you Greek?" Jackson asked as he took his glass. "Don't you usually drink ouzo?"

"*Also* an abomination," Alexis said with a conspiratorial twinkle in his eye. "Have you ever tried the stuff? It's *disgusting*."

"I guess if you don't like black licorice, it might not be for you," Jackson agreed. "But vodka? I can live with that."

He held up his glass, and Alexis clicked it against his own. "To new friendships," Jackson said, eying the very cute man over the rim of his vodka. "And fresh beginnings."

Yes, theoretically Alexis was going to be gone soon, out of Los Angeles, and headed towards Texas, a state that Jackson had sworn he would never return to, but this was why he'd always loved New Year's Eve, right? It was practically part of the holiday mandate to forget all about your inhibitions.

Alexis took a drink of the vodka. "Not bad," he said.

"There's some decent distilleries down in Texas," Jackson said, and then realized, taking a sip out of his own glass, that Alexis hadn't told him yet that he was just passing through or that Texas was his ultimate destination.

Well, *shit*. He was so out of practice at this.

Alexis set his glass down on the bar. His eyes met Jackson's gaze. Jackson had always believed that eyes didn't *twinkle*—that the term was just an invention of overly imaginative writers—but he was taken aback as Alexis' dark eyes actually fucking *twinkled*. Actual heart eyes directed right at Jackson.

"You've been asking around about me," Alexis said, sounding very pleased about this discovery.

Jackson flushed. "You know Tony. He never shuts up."

"Yeah, I do," Alexis said. He leaned in a fraction, and Jackson's heart sped up a little. "I also know he's been recruiting everyone to try to get me to stay. Is that what you are, Jackson Finley, one of Tony's recruits?"

"He might have mentioned it to me," Jackson said. "But no, I'm . . ." *God*, he was so out of practice at this. Just five years ago, he'd have had Alexis charmed and eating out of the palm of his hand. "I'm not here for him, if that's what you're worried about."

"I'm not worried," Alexis said, not sounding like he was. "I know what I want."

"Texas?" Jackson raised an eyebrow. He tossed back the rest of his vodka, feeling the alcohol begin to swirl warmly in his stomach.

"That's why I left Portland," Alexis said. "Well, that and all the rain. It's gonna be nice to go somewhere I can have a year-long season instead of closing up in November and not opening up again til May."

Tony had mentioned how successful Alexis had been in Portland—which Jackson wasn't surprised about in the least, because his food was extraordinary—and that he'd become famous enough that the collective in Austin had literally recruited him.

"Six months off?" Jackson probably would have been climbing the walls if he'd been forced to take that much time off. He had trouble taking a single evening off these days. If only his younger, much more carefree self could see him now, he thought wryly.

"You can technically be open, it's just harder. I can still find some places with decent cover, on the weekends," Alexis confessed. "But it's a waste. Maybe Portland is the food truck capital of the world, but I was ready to move on. When the collective in Austin offered me the spot—they're the top collective in Austin, and it was a big deal to get it—it was a no-brainer."

"So that's why you're here, just for the winter." Jackson was beginning to put together a more accurate picture of Alexis—and maybe he wasn't as much of a workaholic as Jackson was, but he was hardly a slouch either.

"Passing through for a few months. I'd met Tony before, and he offered to help me find some spots here, while I was at a loose end. The collective I'm joining doesn't open until after the holidays. Mid-January, usually."

"That was nice of him," Jackson said, and wondered what Tony's ulterior motive was because he wasn't usually what Jackson would call *nice*.

"Right?" Alexis leaned against the bar, his slender, muscled arm nearly brushing Jackson's. "He's not usually that nice?"

"Have you ever been to Texas?" Jackson asked, suddenly thinking of what Tony had suggested he do. *You can convince him to stay here with us,* Tony had said.

At the time he'd written it off, because it wasn't his place to convince anyone to stick around where they didn't want to be. But why wouldn't LA do just as well as Austin? Tony was starting his own food truck collective. Maybe it wasn't as prestigious as the one Alexis had been invited to in Texas—and Jackson had to wonder if that mattered.

That doesn't matter. If he's a snob, he's still cute enough to warm your bed for New Year's Eve.

"No," Alexis said with a grin. "Will I like it?"

Jackson flushed again. If he'd been asking Tony about Alexis, then Alexis had clearly been asking people about him. "I don't know," he answered honestly, which would probably make Tony screech with frustration if he could hear. "I didn't live in a big city, and I moved away ten years ago. It might be different."

"Why did you move away?" Alexis asked, gesturing to Shaw. He approached, already reaching for the same bottle he'd poured from earlier. He watched as his brother refilled their glasses and then shot Jackson a knowing look.

It was still only nine, and the entire bar probably knew that Jackson was finally going to hook up with someone again. He'd be embarrassed except that Alexis was so hot and so charming, it was hard to feel an ounce of shame that he was lucky enough to be the guy Alexis wanted.

"My dad asked me to come work for him," Jackson said. "And honestly, being gay in a small town in Texas wasn't exactly a fun time."

Alexis nodded, his eyes soft and sympathetic. "I bet not."

"Anyway, my parents got divorced a long time ago, and I never really saw him much, but when he offered me a way out, I took it. Didn't look back."

"And Shaw?"

"He came out a year later. Turns out that it isn't much easier being bi in a small town in Texas," Jackson said dryly.

"Shaw mentioned his dad left him this bar—he left it for both of you?"

"Yeah, we own it together," Jackson said.

"Then why do you do all the work?" Alexis asked in a teasing voice. "I hear all these rumors that you're a workaholic, never leave your office."

"All untrue," Jackson said, "everyone just wants to malign my reputation."

"Right," Alexis said, his eyes twinkling again. He was a literal heart eyes emoji, and Jackson experienced a momentary burst of shocking disappointment. He wanted to enjoy this evening, but it was hard when he kept thinking, *this is really great, but I think I want more?*

But Tony's nudging notwithstanding, Jackson already knew that wasn't going to be possible. He wasn't going to convince Alexis to stay in Los Angeles, not when the only persuasive reason he had was, *we might be something, if you stayed.*

The *might* in that sentence was the kicker. He worked too much and knew it. And frankly, *Alexis* even knew it, and it sounded like Alexis was hardly a slouch either. After all, he was literally running his food truck *by himself* when he was in Los Angeles. So the chances of them being able to make a relationship work, if they even made it that far, were slim.

It wasn't enough—not even close to enough—to ask Alexis to stay in LA.

"How about we toast to a break from reality?" Jackson said, pushing all his melancholy thoughts away. This was New Year's Eve, and if he was really lucky, and played all his cards right, he might get to put his hands and his mouth all over this gorgeous creature in front of him.

"I like that," Alexis said, raising his glass. "To tonight, and to whatever the New Year brings us."

Jackson tipped the vodka back, feeling the burn all the way down his throat. "We should get another drink," he said, "and go see the fire pit. Have you been out to the back patio yet?"

"Yes," Alexis said seriously, "but not with you."

Jackson didn't know if the sudden swooping of his stomach was because of the vodka or Alexis' words. "We'd better remedy that, then," he said. He reached behind the bar and grabbed a bottle. Not the same vodka they'd been drinking, but something else.

"I think," he continued, twisting the top off, "that we better introduce you to one of the best distilleries in Texas."

"What is it?" Alexis asked as Jackson poured them each half a glass. In his defense, he thought, they were going outside, and wouldn't be back anytime soon for a refill.

Or maybe he wanted to get them both a little drunk—not ridiculously drunk, but tipsy enough that it would be easy to just lean in at midnight and kiss him, and then, if that was good, lead Alexis back to his office and the convenient couch in there.

"Tito's," Jackson said, returning the bottle. Resisting the urge to take it with them. "Come on," he said, and to his own surprise, Alexis picked up his glass with one hand and tucked the other behind Jackson's back, underneath his jacket, fingers lightly skimming the fabric of his t-shirt. It was barely a touch, but it felt like a brand, burning right to his skin.

You haven't done this nearly enough recently, if he's affecting you this strongly, Jackson told himself as they walked outside. Alexis' hand hovered right where it had settled, sending little shock waves of sensation through Jackson every time his fingertips brushed his back.

But he was already wondering if it wasn't his admittedly long dry spell, but just the man himself.

There was already a group of guys outside, gathered around the main fire pit, but before Jackson could suggest they find a quieter corner, Alexis had already led him in that direction, towards the secondary, smaller fire, and its empty bench.

They sat down, Alexis' arm still draped across Jackson's back, his fingers grazing his shoulder.

"This is good," Alexis said, taking a drink of vodka. "Really good, in fact."

"Austin is a great city," Jackson said, aware that if Tony could hear him, he'd be swearing right now. Aware that he should be swearing at *himself.* "I think you're going to like it there."

"Really?" Alexis sounded surprised, the edges of his eyes crinkling with amusement. "I thought you weren't such a fan of Texas."

"Austin will be different," Jackson said. "And I bet you'll love their food scene. And they'll love you right back."

"You sound pretty sure of this," Alexis pointed out.

"I've eaten your food, haven't I? Best Greek food I've ever eaten—if I didn't know any better, I'd assume you have little Greek angels in your truck, making it."

"They're there," Alexis said, laughing, and then pointed to his head. "They're all in here. My grandmother, my great-aunt, my sister. They taught me everything I know before they passed. And now, I give their gifts to the world."

"Is that why you started the food truck? You wanted to share your family recipes?" There was no reason to ask the question—Alexis seemed to be on the same page, which was the one-night-stand page, and there was no real reason to share histories or hopes or dreams or any of that. They could just flirt and kiss and then hook up and then it would be over. Maybe it would be easier, in the end, if they hadn't begun to know each other.

"Yes," Alexis said, nodding. "And I love to cook, but I didn't want to go to cooking school. I already *knew* how to cook, and I suppose I could've worked in restaurants, but that didn't appeal to me. Who wants to be yelled at constantly?"

So many of Shaw's food truck friends had told similar stories; they'd wanted to cook but hadn't wanted to be tied down by the chef hierarchy or a brick-and-mortar restaurant.

"Not me," Jackson said. "I don't enjoy *doing* it either, so I don't. I let Shaw handle the kitchen side of the bar."

"You guys serve a pretty decent menu," Alexis said warmly, and maybe it was bullshit—Jackson had eaten Alexis' food and it far surpassed anything that Jackson knew the bar kitchen produced—but it was a nice compliment. One that he was going to take.

"I suppose you wouldn't be interested in parting with your hummus recipe? Once you leave for Austin?" Jackson asked hopefully.

Alexis laughed, and his gaze was a caress along Jackson's face. "Sorry. It's a longtime family secret. Not even for you, Jackson."

"I could trade you for our zucchini fries recipe," Jackson teased. "It's *not* a family recipe, but I'm convinced it's a major reason why we have a solid four-point-eight rating on Yelp."

"They're delicious, but that's not why." Alexis' teasing voice had morphed into something more serious. "It's because you've built a great place here. Good food. Decent priced drinks. A real camaraderie. It's a nice, clean, *safe* place. You should be proud."

Jackson blushed. He rarely considered *why* he worked so goddamn hard. Why it was so vitally important that he take care of everything that cropped up. He kept a lot of his attention on the budget and the income statements because numbers weren't ever his strong suit and he wanted something that would stick around for a long time—long after he and Shaw were gone. But he also wanted what Alexis had said: a nice, clean, safe place. And it often took money to make that possible.

"Thanks," he said. "It means . . . well, it means a lot."

"Truthfully," Alexis said, "places like the Funky Cup sometimes make me rethink my stance on planting roots and growing a business."

Jackson's heart beat faster. Alexis wasn't saying he was *staying*, only that he occasionally wanted to, but *God*, he could think of how it could be.

He'd be less of a recluse, hiding out in his office. Alexis might stop by once or twice a day, dropping a kiss across his lips, reminding him to raise his head, to eat, to *live*.

Jackson knew then that even if Alexis went to Austin, and they never saw each other again, he couldn't go back to the existence he'd had before—because that was all it had been.

It was New Year's Eve, and a night for promises, some of them for your friends and your family, but mostly, it was for promises made to yourself. And Jackson was making some of his own: he was going to start living more and working less. He was going to remodel his house. He was going to take a vacation. He might even start dating again.

It probably wouldn't be Alexis he'd be dating, but Jackson told himself that was okay.

"I always feel like the traditional kind of resolutions are a bad idea, because they add too much pressure," Jackson said. "But what are some promises you'd like to make to yourself?"

"For the New Year?" Alexis leaned back, eyes drifting to the lights ahead, expression thoughtful. "I want to give myself permission to indulge in things I want, even if, on the surface, they look risky."

"Like moving to Austin?" What Jackson really wanted to believe was that Alexis was talking about *him*. But he was almost definitely talking about the big life change he was embarking on this upcoming year.

Alexis tilted his head. "A little like that, yes," he said. Which wasn't really an answer. "What about you?"

"You said you'd heard I work all the time." Jackson took a deep sigh, realizing it was harder to admit this than he'd thought. "I do. And I don't want to, not anymore. It's time to stop living to work and start working to live."

"So you're going to promise yourself not to work so hard?"

"And to do the things I've been putting off," Jackson said.

"How about we start here?" Alexis' voice was soft and rough, like velvet, and he leaned in.

Jackson realized a second before it happened that Alexis was going to kiss him. And he wanted it, wanted it to be the thing he was doing that he'd been putting off for too long.

"I should've done this," Alexis said quietly, lips only a breath away from Jackson's, "that night you looked so tired. I couldn't decide which I wanted to do more: feed you or kiss you." His hand brushed Jackson's face, skimming over his cheekbones, his forehead, under his eyes. "You looked totally worn out, and I wanted to make your life easier, if only for a moment."

Jackson smiled. Couldn't help himself. Alexis' eyes were dark and sweet, brimful of the kind of caring that he hadn't felt in forever from someone who wasn't related to him. Shaw cared, because they were brothers. But nobody else had.

"You did," Jackson said. "You really did."

Chapter Three

Alexis' kiss was soft and gentle, not exactly hesitant, but careful. Like the composition of lips and tongue and mouth was of vital importance, and he didn't want to mess it up. But Jackson slid into the kiss without thinking, and felt his mind go blank, heat pulsing through him at the thought of doing this more, of making Alexis lose his focus, derail his train of thought, burn through his careful self-control.

But there was plenty of time for that later. They had a whole evening ahead of them. And when Jackson broke the kiss, nibbling a little on Alexis' bottom lip as he pulled away, he felt a bone-deep satisfaction as Alexis groaned in his throat.

"It was the best food I've ever eaten," Jackson admitted. "Maybe it was because I was so hungry and tired and at the end of my rope, but you were like . . . a lifeline."

"Is that why you let me kiss you?" Alexis wondered with a fierce, wild grin.

"*Let you kiss me*," Jackson muttered, shooting the other man a teasing glare. "Like I wasn't dying for it the whole damn time."

"Really?" Alexis' face brightened.

"Well, *duh*," Jackson said.

"I'm really glad," Alexis said. "Because I'm probably going to do it again."

"You've got blanket permission," Jackson said. He raised his empty glass, noticing that Alexis' was empty too. "I'm going to get us a refill," he said. "I think we should try another one of your Austin distilleries. You game?"

"Anything you want is fine by me," Alexis said, and Jackson deeply, sincerely hoped that was true, because by the end of the night, he wanted them to be pressed up together, losing count of the number of kisses they shared. He wanted to strip Alexis out of that shirt, one button at a time, wanted to press his palm against the bulge in his jeans, and feel it twitch against his touch.

Jackson stood and, grabbing their glasses, went back into the bar, feeling his skin hum with the electricity between them. He lifted the pass-through, ducking beneath it.

Shaw was making drinks with quick hands, and a slow, easy smile. "How's it going?" he asked. "You guys disappeared, so I figured . . . must be going at least decently."

"He's nice," Jackson said. *And cute. And funny. And sweet. And started his food truck to honor his family.* "I like him."

"You do know . . ." Shaw warned.

"He's not sticking around?" Jackson said, lifting an eyebrow as he pulled the bottle he wanted from the shelf. "Yeah, I know. But that's okay. I'm okay with that." *Except I'm not. I'm really not.*

Shaw caught sight of the bottle in Jackson's hand. "Deep Eddy?"

"I figured we could try all the Austin distilleries," Jackson said.

"It's a little weird that he's trying to go to the one place you swore you'd never go back to," Shaw pointed out as he set a pair of drinks on the bar and pocketed the tip the guy had left him. "Definitely ironic."

Jackson poured the vodka into their glasses, and then returned the bottle to its rightful place on the shelf. "You're telling me," he said. "But Austin is different. And he'll be in a good community."

"Not as good as this one," Shaw said, and Jackson didn't want him to be right, but he probably was.

"Yeah, but is that a good enough reason for me to try to get him to change his mind? We barely know each other."

"You know each other well enough that you want to suck his dick," Shaw teased, pulling a beer, setting the glass down and then pulling another.

Jackson rolled his eyes. "I don't have to know him at all to want to do that."

"True," Shaw admitted. "But you *could* get to know him better. That's a good reason for him to stay."

"And what if it doesn't work out?" Jackson asked incredulously. "Am I supposed to derail his life and plans for the vague possibility that we might date, based on a great conversation and an even better kiss? I don't think so."

Shaw patted him on the back as Jackson pulled the pass-through back up. "Making quick work, huh? Good job, bro."

Jackson didn't bother answering, just picked up the two drinks and went to find his date.

Because that was what it was, wasn't it? A *date*.

It hadn't started out that way, but looking back, Alexis had probably come here, looking for him. And had he been looking for Alexis? Maybe. He'd definitely been looking for something, and he just hoped, deep down, that what he really wanted wasn't exactly what Shaw had been suggesting: a reason for Alexis to stick around.

When Jackson went back outside, Alexis was still lounging on the same bench. The main fire pit had gathered almost twice as many people, but over by the smaller one, Alexis had kept anyone else away.

Jackson had to wonder what he'd said to prevent everyone from crashing their little cozy twosome.

"What's this?" Alexis asked, grinning as Jackson tucked himself back in next to him. This time it felt natural to let Alexis' arm drape across his shoulders and to fill the space that already felt like his.

Jackson handed one of the glasses to him. "Deep Eddy," he said. "I know, I know, flavored vodka can be iffy, but just trust me on this one."

Alexis raised an eyebrow. "I said I would. But ruining good vodka?"

Raising his own glass to his lips, Jackson took a sip. It was just as good and refreshing as he'd remembered—just the slightest hint of fresh grapefruit. So much of the time, flavored vodkas tasted fake, but this one? It tasted *real*.

"Oh, that *is* pretty good," Alexis said after taking a drink. "I really like that."

"Told you," Jackson said, a little smugly.

"They make this in Austin?" Alexis asked, swirling the lightly ruby-colored liquid in his glass. "Maybe I *will* like Texas."

"They've got other flavors too," Jackson pointed out.

"Then," Alexis said conspiratorially, "we'll have to try them all. To celebrate the move."

"Alright," Jackson said. "But first . . ." He leaned in and, this time, when he kissed Alexis, it wasn't just the astringent taste of vodka on his tongue, but the deep citrus of grapefruit, and underneath it, something deeper, darker, almost woodsy. A flavor that belonged to Alexis alone.

Alexis groaned into his mouth as he deepened the kiss, framing Jackson's face with his big, capable hands. "I think," he said, when he pulled back, "I think my *ya-ya* would have liked you very much."

"Your *ya-ya*?" Jackson felt drunk; maybe a little on vodka. Definitely on Alexis' kisses.

"My grandmother," Alexis explained.

"She'd like me because I kissed you?" Jackson took another drink of vodka, but the grapefruit still didn't chase away Alexis' flavor. He still wanted more. He wanted to climb into Alexis' lap and press his cock against Alexis' and let the pleasure just carry them both away. But there were way too many people out here, and glancing at his watch, he knew it was still early yet. Only just ten. It somehow felt unfair to cut their date short of midnight, even though desire was already thrumming, hot and heady, through his blood.

"She would have liked you because you're sweet. Kind. Generous," Alexis said, fingers running through Jackson's hair, smoothing it back from his face. "And you are all those things with me."

"I haven't . . ." Jackson said, flustered. They barely knew each other. His brain kept telling him that, but his heart was already yearning for more of the man next to him.

"You have," Alexis said firmly. "Sometimes you look at someone and you just *know*," he added. "I know you felt it, when you came to my truck."

"Is that why you fed me dinner?" Jackson asked.

"I fed you because you came to the truck," Alexis said with a wry smile.

"I mean . . . you picked out what I wanted, you didn't even wait for me to order."

Alexis shrugged. "I wanted you to have a little of everything that was best. And you liked it."

"I loved it," Jackson admitted. "Are you really sure you won't share your hummus recipe with me?"

Alexis laughed. "How about I tell you a little trade secret? Since my *ya-ya* would've liked you?"

"A hummus trade secret?"

"Yes," Alexis said with a decisive nod. "The trick is you peel the chickpeas."

"Peel them?" Jackson didn't think he even knew what a chickpea looked like. "That's what hummus is made out of, right? Chickpeas?"

"You really don't know much about Greek food, do you?"

"I know I like to eat it," Jackson teased.

"Well, yes, so you take the chickpea after you boil it," Alexis said, miming holding a small pebble-sized object with his fingers, "and then you squeeze it out of the skin. Should come off, easy-peasy."

"You do that to *all* your chickpeas?" Alexis had acted like it was no big deal, but Jackson had a vague idea of how many chickpeas it would take to make the vats and vats of hummus that he probably sold, and the idea of peeling all those chickpeas? It was beginning to dawn on Jackson that he might not be the only workaholic around.

"It's not so bad," he said. "And it's worth it, isn't it?"

Jackson nudged him, loving the way Alexis smiled down at him, fond and amused. "Are you fishing for compliments again?"

"No," Alexis said confidently. "I know my hummus is the best around. Besides, it's a great way to catch up on my binge watching."

"You peel your chickpeas in front of the TV?" If anyone was fond and amused, it was definitely Jackson. But then, he was in the middle of a crush so sudden yet spellbinding that probably anything about Alexis would've looked good right now.

"Where else should I be peeling them?" Alexis wondered.

He had a good point. "I can't believe I never asked this, but where are you staying, while you're here?"

"Don't laugh, but with Tony's . . . um, his brother? Yes, with Wyatt, his brother, he has this huge house, and there's a little guest cottage in the back. And he offered it to me for the time I was here."

"You're staying at Ryan Flores' house?" Jackson wasn't sure why he'd be laughing. Instead, he was actually fairly impressed.

"Who is Ryan Flores?" Alexis asked, and *then* Jackson burst into laughter.

"He plays for the Dodgers." Alexis still looked confused. "The baseball team? Well, Tony's brother, Wyatt, is married to him. So yeah, that's their house.

"You should invite me over sometime. You know, before you go," Jackson continued, then paused, awkwardly, as he realized how that sounded. Maybe they wouldn't be hanging out again, after tonight was over. But just the thought *ached*.

So much potential, and none of it was ever going anywhere.

Jackson finished his glass of vodka, tossing the rest back, and watched as Alexis savored his last sip.

"We should . . ." Jackson stood and gestured towards the bar. It was getting chillier. He could hear the music from out here, as the DJ really got going with the dance music. They rarely had dancing at the Funky Cup, but it was a special night and Jackson had made an exception. And frankly, if he stayed out here with Alexis, cuddling up with him, continuing to kiss and share all kinds of special things, by the end of the night and the time they got naked, his crush was going to be unmanageable.

It was already heading to that point, and they'd barely begun.

But maybe if he could keep it physical . . . could pull Alexis tightly against him, could keep their conversations short, could keep everything but his hands to himself . . . then maybe it wouldn't be so hard to not see him in the morning.

"You want to go inside?" Alexis sounded surprised.

"I know I'd like to dance with you," Jackson said, and that was honest. Maybe not the entire truth, but as much of it as he could share without breaking down and suggesting to Alexis that he should stay.

"I'd love to," Alexis said, standing up and taking Jackson's hand, intertwining their fingers together.

"And," Jackson added, "we can try another flavor of vodka, if you'd like."

"I would," Alexis agreed, "but first, one last thing, before we go inside."

That was all the warning Jackson got before Alexis was tugging him closer, pulling him against his own body, pressing their mouths together in a deeply passionate kiss.

They'd kissed twice before, but this time Jackson was lost in it.

The bar disappeared, the stubborn three cents he hadn't been able to reconcile this week, the vendor who wouldn't renegotiate a raised price, Shaw's annoying habits, everyone who was outside and probably watching them. It all fell away, and the world shrunk down to Alexis: his strong arms wrapping around him, those clever hands trailing up his spine to his neck, and *God*, his mouth—hot and needy, his control beginning to slip as Jackson let loose his own self-control. His cock, hard and ready, brushed against Alexis' thigh, and for a second, he nearly suggested that they go into his office *now*, because he didn't understand the point in waiting. This was happening. They were *going* to have sex at some point, probably in the very near future, and Jackson's entire body didn't know why it wasn't going to happen as soon as possible.

But his heart stopped him from saying it.

It was stupid. He *knew* it was stupid. That was what this really was—a hot New Year's Eve hookup. The problem was that Jackson already knew it could be more, if Alexis wasn't planning on moving a thousand miles away to a state that Jackson had refused to ever visit again.

Alexis lifted his head, his mouth red and wet, and Jackson felt it punch, viscerally, through him. But he resisted, because what if it was over the moment after they'd both gotten off? He already knew that morning was going to bring an ugly kind of clarity, but he wasn't ready to face it yet. Not while it was still dark, and there was still time.

Chapter Four

The crowd inside the Funky Cup had doubled since Jackson had been in for refills.

"Another drink?" Alexis asked, his voice soft but rough, hovering right above Jackson's ear.

Jackson nodded. "I'll grab us some," he said. The bar was packed, and Shaw and the other two bartenders were hopping. He set the two empties in the very full tray, noticed that they were running low on clean glassware, and decided he would help out by running a load through the under-counter dishwasher. He filled up the tray the rest of the way, and then sliding it into the dishwasher, started it.

When he looked up, it was undeniable that everyone clamoring for a drink was going to be waiting a while. And *yes*, he was not supposed to be working, but what was he supposed to do? Let people go thirsty at his bar on New Year's Eve?

For the next ten minutes, Jackson poured drinks and took cash and hoped that Alexis would understand that sometimes work obligations superseded just about everything else. Especially when those work obligations were thirty or so very thirsty gays who *needed* their holiday booze.

When the main lineup at the bar cleared, Jackson glanced up and saw Alexis standing to the side, sipping a glass of something, seemingly patiently waiting for him to finish up.

After Jackson had caught his eye, Alexis smiled and then approached the now much less crowded bar. "For a second I thought I lost you," he said seriously, "and I was heartbroken. But then I realized you just needed to take care of something, and then you'd be free."

As if Jackson needed any more evidence that Alexis would be a great boyfriend for a guy like him, who sometimes had shit that needed done and had to take the time to do it. He'd be understanding, but he wouldn't let Jackson lose himself in the work, either.

Maybe it would take a little practice, but they'd find a good balance.

Or they would have, if this didn't have to come to an inevitable conclusion.

"I'm glad you waited," Jackson said, grabbing himself a fresh glass. "Did you get a drink?"

"Oh, yeah, Shaw poured it for me. Said I'd like the orange flavor, and I do. It's really good."

"Not as good as the grapefruit, but yeah, still really good," Jackson agreed. He poured himself some, adding a splash of soda, if only because if they kept going like this, he was going to be incoherent by midnight. What he wanted was to be buzzed, not drunk. He wanted to remember every single thing about what happened after the ball dropped, because the chances of it happening again were so damn small.

Jackson already knew that he was going to want to savor every single moment.

He took a sip and yeah, that *was* good. Alexis' face crinkled into a smile. "You're cute," he said, as Jackson opened the pass-through and let himself out from behind the bar.

"Trust me," Jackson said, laying a hand on Alexis' chest, "not as cute as you are. How are you even real?"

Alexis pinched himself in the arm. "Feel real," he said, laughing. "But honestly, why'd we wait til now?"

Jackson knew the answer to that question—he worked so hard that he rarely even noticed what was going on around him—and he also knew that deep down, there was a part of him that was glad they hadn't really met before tonight. Yes, more time with Alexis would have been extraordinary, but then again, it would have been *undeniably* extraordinary, thus making it even harder to say goodbye when the time came. Jackson probably would have ended up with a full-fledged broken heart, instead of the mildly bruised one he'd already resigned himself to.

"Probably because I work too hard?" Jackson said, raising an eyebrow. The music had gotten louder. He took a long drink from his glass, and then taking his own, and also Alexis', set them around the corner of the bar where Shaw would know not to touch them. Shed his jacket. "Come on," he said, taking his hand and tugging him toward where the dancing had begun, "I've earned a little respite, don't you think?"

"More than a little," Alexis said earnestly, but followed so docilely Jackson almost forgot for a minute that he could be forceful too. But then Jackson turned around and, suddenly, Alexis' hands were all over him, pulling him in, fingers tightening on his hips as they began to move with the beat of the music and Jackson nearly groaned. Why did this man have to be so goddamned perfect? It was like he was a challenge from fate, hand-delivered to his doorstep, trying to make his life both way better and way harder.

"I like you like this," Alexis said, nuzzling into his ear, Jackson barely able to discern his words. "So sexy when you let go."

And he *wanted* to let go. He wanted to walk to the edge of the cliff, hold his arms out, and let himself fall, knowing that Alexis would catch him.

Jackson shook his head briefly, trying to clear the undoubtedly alcohol-induced fantasies from it. There was going to be no falling. This was supposed to be a night of fun, and he was *having* fun. He should enjoy it, instead of mooning after things he couldn't have.

So he swung his hips, getting into the beat, feeling Alexis' fingers grasp his hips, rubbing his ass rather shamelessly against the other man's hardening cock.

It had already been a good night. The drinks, the company, the man behind him. Jackson already knew he wanted Alexis to fuck him, and if Alexis was going to be on board, then it was going to be an even better one.

He'd make him feel good—Jackson knew that, and it made him trust Alexis in a way he hadn't trusted anyone in a very long time.

They danced for a while longer, then took a break, Alexis' shirt riding up as he wiped his sweat-damp forehead with his sleeve. Just a glimpse of his toned torso had Jackson nearly choking on his vodka. He wanted to put his hands and his mouth all over his skin and all the muscles rippling underneath. Especially on the trail of dark hair that led underneath the waistband of his jeans. Definitely on the hard bulge underneath the zipper.

Jackson swallowed his vodka. It might've burned, but it was hard to tell under all the arousal surging through him. He glanced at his watch. It was just past eleven. He'd promised himself he wouldn't pull Alexis in the direction of his office until midnight had struck, but maybe . . .

"Hey, I see you two found each other, finally."

Jackson glanced up and Tony Blake was standing there, arm casually draped around his boyfriend's set of muscular shoulders. Lucas was barely wearing a shirt, and maybe in another time, Jackson might have enjoyed the view, but tonight, all he could see was Alexis. His tall, rangy build. His own slightly less obvious muscles. The kind, unbelievably sexy earnestness in his dark eyes. Jackson had never imagined that someone being genuine could be such an incredible turn-on, but it was—though he wasn't sure it would work that well on anybody but Alexis.

"Yeah, we did," Jackson said, wondering just how much of a matchmaking job Tony was doing here. And was he doing it because he genuinely wanted Jackson to find happiness? Or because Tony wanted Alexis to stay in LA and join his own food truck collective that'd be opening in a few months? When it came to Tony, it was hard to say. Shaw would have told him he was overthinking it, and if there were multiple benefits to multiple people, didn't that make everything better, in the end? Jackson wasn't quite sure that he'd have agreed.

"I'm glad," Tony said, sounding like he genuinely meant it. And he probably did. For multiple reasons. He turned to Alexis. "You given any more thought to my proposal?"

Alexis nodded, and Jackson wished they were alone so he could ask if it was what he thought it was. Tony would tell him, too, if he wanted to know, but Jackson wasn't sure he was interested in cluing Tony into his undeniable fascination with the other food truck owner.

"I have," Alexis said. "And I'm still thinking about it."

Yeah, all that measured thoughtfulness was definitely more attractive on Alexis than it would be on just about anyone else. Jackson was becoming fairly certain of that fact.

"Course," Tony said. "No reason to rush."

"The situation is a bit fluid," Alexis admitted.

Jackson took another drink and told himself he was not dying to know what they were talking about. *Nope, definitely not.*

"I bet it is," Tony said, finishing his beer. He turned to Lucas. "Care to grab us another round?" he said.

"For you, maybe," Lucas retorted fondly. "But I'm driving home."

The mushy way that Tony stared at his boyfriend made Jackson feel not only impatient to know what Alexis was thinking about, but impatient to find someone of his own. Someone he could love the way that Tony and Lucas loved each other.

You have, that annoying voice insisted, *and he's standing right next to you.*

Jackson tossed back the rest of his vodka, hoping that at least would silence the knowing voice that seemed to understand his heart better than he did.

"Let's try the cranberry, this time," Jackson said, and reached behind the bar, plucking the bottle out of the lineup without really looking.

Evidence that he really didn't spend as much time behind the bar as Shaw did? Additional evidence that he'd already had too many shots of vodka? The fact that he'd pulled the birthday cake vodka out of the lineup instead of the Deep Eddy he'd been aiming for.

Alexis raised a dark eyebrow. He seemed amused. "Birthday cake?"

Jackson countered him with an eyebrow raise of his own. He'd definitely had too much vodka if birthday cake was sounding appealing. "You game to give it a go?"

Alexis shrugged. "Why not?"

"Oh, I *have* to see this," Tony said, rubbing his hands with excitement. "Al must really be sweet on you if he's willing to drink *flavored* vodka."

"Birthday cake-flavored vodka, no less," Lucas said, handing his boyfriend a fresh pint.

Jackson grabbed two shot glasses, splashed some vodka in, and handed one to Alexis.

"You should probably get some kind of reward for drinking this," he said right after he tossed it back, the sickly sweet taste enveloping his tastebuds. "That's kind of . . . well, *ew*."

"Hey, you stock that at *your* bar," Tony pointed out, chuckling.

But Alexis' eyes were calm and radiant still, focused only on Jackson's face. He cupped his cheeks with his two big hands, and said, very seriously, "I do," before leaning in and kissing him.

Jackson was not usually a fan of demonstrations of affection in public, but there was something about Alexis' slow, sweet, deeply serious kisses that not only undid him, they undid all his previous opinions.

If Alexis was going to keep kissing him, then Jackson was definitely going to keep letting him.

Tony whooped a little, which broke the spell, and Jackson pulled away.

"That's it," Tony said, clearly amused, "I think you guys have definitely had enough to drink."

Jackson glared at him. "Maybe, maybe not," he said, though this time when he grabbed a glass, he filled it with water, gulping down half and sharing it with Alexis, who took it with a quiet look of gratitude.

"Come on," Lucas said, tugging on his boyfriend's arm. "Leave them alone and dance with me."

Tony had never needed persuading to put *his* hands all over Lucas, especially in a public place, so a moment later, Jackson was alone again with Alexis. Alone, if you didn't count all the people rapidly cramming their way into the Funky Cup.

"You want to dance again?" Alexis asked, leaning in very close so Jackson could hear him. It *had* gotten louder.

Jackson was tempted to tell him to forget this, that they could go *really* be alone some place, and that place wasn't his office but his house.

Was he really considering bringing Alexis home with him?

Jackson discovered that he was. He thought about how much more comfortable they'd be in his bed. He thought about the way Alexis would look in his shower, naked and soapy. He thought about a midnight snack in his kitchen. He thought about the morning light on Alexis' hair.

The only problem with all of those visions was he'd planned on sleeping the night's partying off on the couch in his office—alone. An Uber or a taxi would be impossible to get right now, considering it was almost midnight, and it was way too far to walk.

"Do you not want to dance with me?" Alexis had a concerned wrinkle between his dark brows, and Jackson realized that he'd never answered his question—he'd been too busy trying to figure out a solution to the problem with all that alcohol surging through his system.

"No, no, of course I do. I do." Jackson glanced at his watch again. Forty-five minutes til midnight.

"Something is on your mind," Alexis said, and *yes*, there was, but the something was not part of the plan. Not even close.

"I was just thinking . . ." Jackson took a deep breath. "You wanna get out of here?"

Alexis' smile was soft. Understanding. Like he'd known what Jackson wanted, before he even wanted it. Which was possible because he'd already done that once before, with the dinner he'd served him.

"I would like that," he said, then his expression turned reluctant. "Where? And how will we get there?"

"My house," Jackson said decisively, before he could change his mind. "And I've got no idea, but we'll figure something out."

"There isn't much time before . . ." Alexis stopped. "And I would very much like to kiss you at midnight, if you are okay with that."

Like they hadn't already kissed half a dozen times this evening. It was endearing and sweet and warmed a corner of Jackson's heart that he hadn't even realized had grown cold—but it had. "Yes. Yes. Definitely. We are going to be kissing at midnight, no question about that."

"Okay. Good. Then I am yours," Alexis said, spreading his hands out, like that was all he cared about: getting a chance to kiss Jackson at midnight. And that cold, long-abandoned place grew a little warmer still.

"I'm going to figure this out," Jackson said with a confidence he did not feel.

He looked around, wondering what he should do—who he could call—when he spotted a person just on their way out, ducking their head slightly like they didn't want to be seen leaving the party early.

Jackson grabbed Alexis' hand and dragged him through the crowd, towards the door, and the person he'd just seen leave.

It had grown colder outside, the air almost crisp even for LA. "Hey," he called to the lone figure walking down the sidewalk. He supposed he couldn't really be surprised that Tate Ward would duck out of the party before midnight. Tony had mentioned that the food truck he owned with his sister had been struggling recently, and weren't all that close to meeting the sales threshold Tony had set to get into the new food truck collective. If Jackson had been Tate, he probably wouldn't feel much like partying either.

Plus, as Tony had mentioned offhandedly the other day, Tate was perennially single, and not really because of a lack of opportunity either. He turned down dates and hookups regularly, almost, Tony had said, like he was waiting for something. Maybe even *someone*. But Jackson didn't know what it was, only that he was a tiny bit grateful that when he needed Tate, he was right there. Alone, and almost certainly persuadable.

Tate turned, his trademark knit cap covering his reddish-brown hair, his gray eyes bleached pale under the light from a nearby streetlamp. "Hey, Jackson," he said as he pulled out his car keys. "Everything alright?"

Jackson nodded, probably a little drunkenly, and more than a little enthusiastically. "It's good. It's really good. I was just wondering . . . can you give us a ride? Back to my place? There's no way we can catch an Uber or a cab right now."

Tate looked really surprised, and Jackson couldn't exactly blame him. When was the last time he'd brought a guy home? He couldn't even remember. Definitely not in the few years Tate had been friends with his brother.

"You want me to give you and Alexis a ride to your house?" Tate did not look convinced.

"I'll persuade Shaw to give you a few more evenings a week on the truck rotation, outside the bar," Jackson said. Yes, he was desperate. No, he did not care if he looked it. Alexis' hand was warm and steady in his own, and it felt like it belonged there, even though that was impossible.

Tate raised a dubious eyebrow. "Doesn't Shaw set the schedule a month in advance?"

"Yes," Jackson said recklessly. "But it's my bar."

Next to him, Alexis chuckled.

"Alright," Tate said, and gestured towards a car that was parked at the curb. "Your chariot awaits."

CHAPTER FIVE

TATE WAS QUIET AFTER he'd gotten Jackson's address and punched it in his GPS. The only sound in the car was the sound of the directions, and occasionally the sound of Alexis' shifting next to him. They'd originally buckled up in the backseat, but Jackson found himself slumping towards Alexis, anyway. Enjoying the feeling of his chest, warm and solid, next to him.

"Seems like it was a pretty good party," Tate said, finally breaking the silence.

Jackson thought it had been, but then Tate couldn't really believe that, because he'd been on his way out the door forty-five minutes before midnight.

"Yeah, it was," Alexis spoke up. "A great party." He glanced over at Jackson, the expression on his face not only fond, but understanding. Like he'd figured out why Tate was leaving what he'd called a "pretty good party" before midnight.

"My sister is home, and I always like to watch the ball drop with her," Tate said, and the edge of his voice was defensive.

Even if he hadn't already promised, Jackson would've decided that moment to work Tate into the schedule more if he could. Shaw liked Tate, a lot. There'd been a point when he'd even hoped that something might happen between his brother and the food truck owner, but they'd never shown any interest in each other.

It was totally none of his business, but Jackson wanted to know what Tate was waiting for.

"Looks like we're almost there," Tate said. Like he was glad. And he probably was, because while this ride had been a godsend, it had also been awkward, *and* Jackson was very ready to be truly alone with Alexis.

"I really appreciate the ride," Jackson said, when Tate pulled over to the curb, right in front of his house. "And I'll talk to Shaw."

"Yes," Alexis said, reaching between the seats and giving Tate a heartfelt clasp on the shoulder. "Thank you. And happy New Year, my friend."

"Yes," Jackson called out as he slid out of the car, Alexis following behind him. "Happy New Year!"

A moment later, Tate drove off with a last wave, and they were alone. *Finally.*

Alexis' arms wrapped around him from behind, his head resting on Jackson's shoulder. "This is your house?" he asked. "It's really sweet."

"It's small," Jackson said, as he reached back and grabbed Alexis' hand. Pulled him towards the front walk. "I also meant, when I bought it, to put some money into it. Update it, some. But . . ."

"You work too much?" Alexis sounded wryly amused. "I had no idea."

Jackson pulled his keys out of his pocket and unlocked the door, swinging it open. He was glad he'd left the small light in the living room on, because it lit up the room just enough. They both took off their shoes, Jackson pulling his own boots off, and Alexis following suit.

The furniture in the living room was from IKEA and nothing to write home about, but Alexis smiled as he glanced around. "This room feels like you," he said.

"Boring? Dismal?" Jackson asked ruefully. The couches were dark gray, the rug charcoal, the throw pillows black and ivory velvet. It had seemed like a good idea to keep to a neutral palate when he'd bought everything because he hadn't known what he was going to do with the house. But now, looking at it through Alexis' eyes, it just looked *boring*.

"Dark colors, but with secret pops of color. That burnt orange chair. The turquoise pillow. The yellow vase," Alexis said firmly, pointing to each object, things that Jackson had collected over the years, things that were meaningful to him, but that he'd never really thought about.

It occurred to him that Alexis really *saw* him in a way that a lot of others didn't, and because that knowledge ached deep inside, he turned towards him and asked, "Do you want a tour?" Really hoping that they could dispense with both the pleasantries and the charade and have sex, before Jackson's crush grew any deeper.

"Honestly?" Alexis' voice was wry. "I was kind of hoping we could start with your bedroom."

It was exactly the answer that Jackson had been hoping for, but he still had to push away a tiny bit of hurt.

Of course Alexis wanted to have sex. *Jackson* wanted to have sex.

He'd been wanting to have sex for so long that when Alexis reached out, his hand wrapping around Jackson's waist, tugging him closer, the heat inside him flared to life almost immediately. And when Alexis leaned down and kissed him firmly, his nimble tongue seeking Jackson's, velvet rough and determined, the fire inside drowned out any last-minute objections.

They'd been heading this way from that moment a week ago, and now it was happening, and Jackson wasn't going to stop them.

He curled his fingers around Alexis' neck and tugged them toward his bedroom. Clearing away some clothes he'd tried on and discarded with one arm, he scooted onto the bed, tugging Alexis closer, but then he broke the kiss, eyes dark and determined as he stared at Jackson.

"What do you want?" Alexis asked.

Jackson's fingers tangled in the silken strands of Alexis' hair that just brushed the top of his neck. He knew what he wanted, but he was painfully unused to asking for it. He hesitated, and Alexis intervened in the sudden silence.

"I want what *you* want, but I also want to make you cry, and then make you beg me to fuck you," Alexis said, voice so steady that Jackson wanted to undo it, wanted to make *him* beg.

But . . . there was also everything *he* wanted, and it just happened to line up with everything Alexis had just said.

It would be stupid to argue when just the words were nearly enough to undo him. "Yes," he said breathlessly. "Yes, to all that."

"Good," Alexis said.

"Side drawer," Jackson said, reaching for the hem of his t-shirt, ready to get naked. He'd been ready to get naked before he'd ever put clothes on today, and then he'd met Alexis, and need had blossomed into something else entirely.

Alexis chuckled, and his hands stopped Jackson's in place, before he could tug his shirt over his head. "Wait," he said. "There's no need to rush."

Then, like he was demonstrating, he pushed Jackson up further onto the bed, climbed on top of him, and kissed him like they had all the time in the world. Hours and hours to work themselves up, until they were close to the breaking point, until Jackson wasn't even sure he remembered his own name.

And they weren't even naked yet.

Alexis was busy nibbling on his neck, slow, drugging kisses that seemed to go on and on, never ending and intoxicating. Jackson's fingers were dug into Alexis' firm, muscular shoulders as he writhed, looking for any kind of relief against his hard, aching cock. Even a single touch might be enough; he was so desperate he might take anything.

Jackson was just about to demand that they do *anything* other than kiss, when Alexis pulled back, resting his weight on his elbows, and just smiled, soft and dreamy. "I really like this," he said.

"Do you?" Jackson's flirtatious banter was terrible, but then it felt like it had been ages since he had *any* blood in his brain, and he was getting a little loopy.

"I like you," Alexis said, still dreamy, and then before Jackson could plead or bargain or beg, Alexis whipped his t-shirt off. Jackson groaned as Alexis' lips coasted lower, creeping down his chest, until they were nibbling on his stomach, leaving an unbroken chain of love bites. The pleasure was intense; the pain just the right counterpoint. Even better, he liked that they might last longer than just tonight. That in the morning, when Alexis was long gone, he might be able to press on each spot, and remember what it had felt like to have Alexis kissing him there.

"I like you, too," Jackson said, "but *God*, if you don't touch me soon, I'm gonna . . ."

He didn't have to actually come up with a threat, because Alexis pressed a palm against his cock, and it twitched, wet and messy, in his boxer briefs. Jackson couldn't swallow back his groan. "Yes," he begged, absolutely shamelessly. "Touch me, suck me, *fuck* me."

Alexis' grin was adorable and also infuriating. "All in good time," he said, and took an *age* unbuttoning and unzipping Jackson's jeans. Then instead of pulling them down, Alexis applied himself to Jackson's feet—a location he'd never considered an erogenous zone in his entire life. But the way Alexis carefully and erotically peeled off his socks? Jackson would be jerking off to that alone for the next fifty years.

Just when Jackson was about to scream with frustration, that was when Alexis removed his jeans, so quickly and efficiently that Jackson had barely blinked and they were gone, discarded on the floor.

What was with this guy? Ten years on taking his socks off and his jeans were gone in a millisecond? Jackson didn't know . . . but he couldn't even finish his thought because then his briefs were off too, and *oh God*, that was Alexis' mouth and it was so hot and wet on his cock, sucking it deep before Jackson could even brace himself for the overwhelming pleasure. Goddamn *moaning* around it, like it was the best thing he had ever put in his mouth.

Jackson's mind was a blank slate, one overriding thought chasing all the others away—if Alexis kept up this fucking incredible suction and the slow tug and pull he was doing on his balls, he was going to come before Alexis' cock got anywhere near his ass. And it had been *so* long. He'd wanted it forever, but hadn't found anyone he'd really wanted to fuck him in an age. But Alexis was different. Alexis redefined everything, despite Jackson's best efforts to keep him nicely boxed up and labeled as "one-night stand."

"Fuck, fuck, you gotta," Jackson managed to say through his moans. "I don't want to come yet."

"Don't worry," Alexis said, all that bountiful confidence still sexy as hell. "You won't."

"I might," Jackson admitted.

Alexis legitimately *pouted* at that. "You deserve all the pleasure in the world, first," he said, stubbornly. "Let me give it to you."

"Why don't we . . ." Jackson gestured between them. "Give each other a little pleasure?" He hoped Alexis would get on with it and begin to prep him to fuck, but they could also cross that bridge in a few minutes—if Jackson could find the self-control to last that long.

Alexis smiled at that suggestion. "Even better."

This time it was Jackson who pulled Alexis' clothes off—but he didn't have the everlasting patience that his lover had, and they were gone fast, Jackson's hands running all over his gloriously naked skin. He was even hotter than Jackson had imagined, so lean, with the longest legs. A torso bunched with muscle that Jackson knew he could spend at least a whole evening on. But they didn't have that kind of time, no matter how much Alexis liked to pretend they did. He pressed one quick, but loving kiss to Alexis' abs, feeling them tense underneath his lips, and then flipped himself around, settling down so his face was hovering right above Alexis' hard cock.

He thought about how much Alexis had teased him, and just let his tongue graze the wet tip, tracing patterns along the underside, feeling the man underneath him quake.

Alexis had returned to his balls, tugging on them exactly the way Jackson liked, sending pleasure through him in jolts.

He was so preoccupied with torturing Alexis the way he'd tortured him, that he must have missed the sound of the drawer opening and closing because suddenly there was something slick and wet sliding alongside his crack, down to his hole, and he nearly choked on Alexis' cock when his thumb unexpectedly skimmed over it, and then sank inside.

Jackson gasped as Alexis' thumb pushed deeper, as his hand continued tugging on his balls, rolling them between his fingers. His cock brushed hot and wet against Alexis' chest but there was almost no pressure against it and he still had to take a deep breath, and then another, trying to get his arousal under control so he could give back to Alexis as good as he was giving to him.

But then, before Jackson could quite master himself, the thumb was gone, and the movement had stopped, and he knew exactly what that meant. He sank down on Alexis' cock, relishing the salty, sweet tang of it in his mouth and was rewarded by not only Alexis' thumb sinking back inside of him, but a second finger too, carefully stretching him as the fingers wiggled deeper, hitting a spot inside of him that nearly made Jackson yell.

But he knew better now, and kept sucking, the feedback loop of pleasure growing until all he knew was the rock-hard cock against his tongue, pushing and pushing as Alexis continued to finger-fuck him mercilessly.

Then suddenly, it ended, leaving Jackson empty. He pulled off Alexis' cock with a breathless, wordless gasp.

"Come here," Alexis said, and this time, his voice didn't sound even or measured or remotely in control. He sounded gravelly and gruff, like he was right on the edge, just like Jackson was.

"Kiss me," he said, when Jackson turned around, taking in his damp face, sweat beaded on his forehead, his dark hair pushed back. Jackson leaned down and kissed him, heard the condom wrapper rip open as he nibbled along Alexis' lower lip.

"Like this," Alexis said as Jackson lifted his head up. "Come on, just like this."

Jackson didn't need any more encouraging. It was a lot of stretch, after so long going without, but Alexis had prepped him well, and as he straddled him and started to fuck down on his cock, he felt him slip in, slowly but surely.

"Goddamn, you feel good," he said, bracing his hands on Alexis' chest, watching as his eyes fluttered closed. When he was fully seated, he let out the breath he hadn't known he was holding. He was so full he felt overwhelmed with it. Reaching down, he grasped his own cock, moaning as he tugged on himself, rocking back and forth on Alexis' dick, feeling the curved end press right into that spot that made him see stars.

"Yeah, yeah," Alexis said, moaning mindlessly right along with him. "Fuck me, baby."

Jackson discovered that was what he wanted more than anything else in the entire world right now. It had narrowed in, focusing on just them, in this bed together.

It had been so long since Jackson had done this, but it turned out that riding a hot guy was just like riding a bike—Jackson remembered almost immediately how to drive the man underneath him crazy, and Jackson right along with him. He felt the pleasure spike through him as he went faster and faster, fucking down on Alexis' cock with determination and drive, his hand cupped only lightly around his own, because just like it felt like he'd been waiting all night to have sex, it felt like he'd been waiting all night to come, and he knew it wouldn't take much. He could almost . . .

Then Alexis reached out, gripping his hips, bouncing him harder and harder, and goddamn, that was hitting him right on the prostate and, *shit*, Jackson suddenly felt the pleasure rising in him in one big wave and he let go of his cock, hoping to forestall it just a moment longer, but it was too late. He was falling off the edge, yelling something, *anything*, and coming in hot, long pulses across Alexis' chest. Slumping down, not even caring about the mess as Alexis gave a yelp of his own, and came right after him.

For a long moment, they didn't move. Jackson wasn't sure he *could* move. That had been . . . *well*, the first sex he'd had in a long time, but he knew it hadn't been so long that he'd forgotten how good it could be. This was definitely the best sex he had ever had.

He squeezed his eyes shut and hoped, almost, that this moment could last longer. That time could draw itself out until Alexis didn't really have to say goodbye at all. They could just stay here, static, and it would never end.

But that was impossible, and he knew it.

"Happy New Year." Alexis' voice was sweet and soft, and he dropped a tender kiss on the top of Jackson's head.

"Is it midnight?" Jackson wondered. Surprised himself at how steady his voice was. He thought it would be all cracked and wrecked, like he felt inside.

How could something be the best night of his life and the worst, all at the same time?

"Does it matter?" Alexis wondered.

"No, not really," Jackson admitted. Maybe he hadn't had his kiss at midnight, but what they'd shared was so much better.

"We should . . ." Alexis said, shifting underneath him. Jackson knew he should move. Should clean up. Should begin the inexorable march to the point where Alexis walked out the door and he never saw him again. If only it wasn't completely totally batshit crazy to ask Alexis to stick around Los Angeles after one date. Admittedly, the best date of his life, despite that it had only been *one date*.

What if things between them didn't work out, and he cost Alexis the chance of a lifetime? The dream of his future? As much as Jackson wanted to say, "Hey, *hypothetically*, how would you feel about staying around so we could do this again? Hopefully lots of times?" he didn't think he could bring himself to be that selfish.

It would be a sweet, romantic gesture at first. But eventually Alexis might come to resent him. Jackson could see it. He could even *feel* it, because work was as important to Alexis as it was to him, and if Alexis ever asked him to give up the bar . . . *well*, that wasn't going to happen.

Jackson might be looking for more of a healthy work-life balance, but he wasn't looking to completely upend his whole life, and he didn't think Alexis was either.

It's just bad timing, he thought, and then revised that statement to, *it's the worst timing ever, in the whole history of timing.*

"We should," Jackson agreed and shifted in bed, Alexis' cock slipping out of him. He stretched his back and finally slid off the bed, his feet landing with a thud on the hardwood floor.

The light in the room was dim, only the lamp in the corner illuminating Alexis' face, but Jackson could've sworn he looked disappointed.

But then the emotion was gone, if Jackson had ever seen it at all, and he turned to go to the bathroom.

The bright light in the bathroom seemed to clear away the last of the alcohol cobwebs from his mind. He knew he wasn't sober, but he *felt* sober. He wet a washcloth, cleaned up, and then pulled another one for Alexis from the cabinet. He was about to turn to go back into the bedroom, but Alexis appeared in the doorway, absolutely, gloriously naked. Sheepishly, he held up the condom he'd just finished tying off.

Jackson gestured towards the little trash can in the corner, and then after he'd disposed of the condom, handed him the damp washcloth.

"Thanks," Alexis said, flashing him a quick, grateful smile after he'd finished wiping off, and Jackson had disposed of both of them in the hamper. "Hey," he said, turning towards Jackson, a deeper, sweeter smile replacing the awkwardness, "are you hungry?"

"I could eat," Jackson said, and then his stomach literally *rumbled*, clear as day in the small bathroom.

Alexis chuckled. "I think you probably could." And before Jackson could say, *let's get dressed and contemplate how this is all going to end,* he was heading out of the bathroom, through the bedroom—*without* grabbing any clothes, either—and into the kitchen.

CHAPTER SIX

JACKSON WATCHED WITH SLIGHT trepidation as he pulled open Jackson's fridge. God only knew what was in there. Probably not much of anything, because as they both knew, Jackson was always at work.

But to his surprise, Alexis emerged with a slightly worse-for-the-wear red bell pepper, half a red onion, eggs, and a hunk of cheese. "The omelet never fails," Alexis said, setting his load on the counter.

Jackson watched with interest as Alexis started rooting around in his cupboards, looking for a frying pan. It was hard *not* to be interested—or to want to cut short his quest by telling him where they were—because Alexis sure had an incredibly fine ass. Pale, maybe, but muscled and firm. Biteable, even. Jackson decided life was incredibly unfair, because he would never get to nibble on that particular muscle.

"You cook," Alexis stated after he'd found the pan and had placed it on the stove, melting a hunk of butter in it.

"Sometimes, yeah, but not as much as I'd like to," Jackson said. "However, breakfast is usually my specialty." It was the one time during the day when he usually wasn't at work, and had the opportunity. Plus, there were all those times he'd cooked breakfast for guys, on their way out the door. Not once had any of them ever cooked for him—and the fact that Alexis was doing it now, naked and without an ounce of shame, was making his chest hurt a little.

Alexis shot him a sly smile. "Maybe you should be making this, then," he said, as one of Jackson's knives cut through the pepper and the onion at a dizzying speed, leaving a perfect dice in its wake.

"I think I'll leave it to the expert. *You*," Jackson said, laughing. "I definitely can't do that."

"Eh, it is not hard. Just many, many hours of practice." He smiled. "But," he added, "the omelet still tastes the same, no matter how flashy your knife skills are."

"Yeah, but I'd be way less impressed," Jackson teased.

Alexis flushed, and Jackson was fairly sure it wasn't just from the heat of the stove as he dumped the vegetables into the pan, and started whisking up the eggs.

"Believe it or not," Alexis said as he shook the pan, and reached for salt and pepper, "I've never cooked naked before."

There was nothing that Jackson wanted more than to reach up and press a palm to the broad plane of Alexis' bare back, feeling the fine grain of his skin. He wanted to turn him around, to kiss him again. But Jackson was afraid that if he did any of those things, he might become officially lost, swamped with something he didn't quite understand. So instead, he kept his distance and tried to focus on the fact that a very hot man was in his kitchen, cooking for him.

It didn't quite work.

Instead, Jackson found himself pulling out orange juice, two glasses, and then plates, silverware, setting the tiny kitchen table like they were having a four-course meal instead of sharing an omelet.

He even dug out a candle, and after setting it in the middle of the table, grabbed his lighter out of the junk drawer and lit it.

When he turned back towards the kitchen, Alexis was lifting the pan off the stove, carrying it towards the table.

"Perfect," he said, neatly slicing the gorgeous omelet in half, and sliding a piece onto each plate.

And as they sat down, Jackson found he couldn't have said it any better himself.

Alexis lifted the glass of juice and Jackson found himself doing the same, indulging in an impromptu toast. "To the best New Year's I've ever had," Alexis said. "Thank you for sharing it with me."

"I . . ." For a split second, Jackson almost considered saying, *Me, too, and guess what? We could do this all the time!* But he didn't, because there was no point in hashing this out when there were still a few hours they could enjoy together. In the end, he just smiled and said, "Me too. It's been great."

Alexis' eyes were warm on his bare chest as he ate his omelet and then leaned back, full and happy and only filled with a tiny bit of regret. This would be a night that he would think about often. Definitely every New Year's. There'd never be any horrible breakup, any words he'd wish he hadn't said, no fights he wanted to take back. They would begin and end, and it would be perfect the whole way through. There was a certain beauty in that, Jackson decided, and that was what he would focus on.

Not the pain and the disappointment and the regret he'd feel when Alexis walked out the front door, but the joy and happiness he'd felt over the last few hours.

Jackson yawned. The evening—and the last few months, likely the last few *years*—were catching up with him. He was tired, even though he didn't want to be.

"It's late," Alexis said then, and all of Jackson's castles in the sky—all the lies he'd told himself so he would be okay with this—collapsed. "It's after one. I could probably get an Uber, head back to the cottage."

"You could always stay the night," Jackson said, hating himself for suggesting it, because if they slept together, everything would only feel worse in the morning.

Alexis tilted his head, considering Jackson, his gaze glued to his face. "I want to," he said finally, "but how much I want to means I probably shouldn't."

"Yeah," Jackson said, swallowing hard, hoping the lump in his throat would disappear. It didn't. "When do you leave for Austin?"

"In a few days, I think," Alexis said. "Maybe a week."

Jackson nearly suggested they meet up again before he left, but he didn't, because if Alexis knew he shouldn't spend the night, going on another date was definitely out of the question. No matter how badly he wanted it.

Alexis rose, and to Jackson's surprise, took his hand, and pressed a firm, warm kiss to the back of it, the chivalrous gesture at odds with his naked self. But then, Jackson thought that he'd never met a man more willing to think of others first. Never met a man who was more a gentleman. "Thank you for such a wonderful evening," he said.

"No, thank *you*," Jackson said, standing with Alexis and following him back into the bedroom where he fetched his phone, called an Uber, and then dressed, slowly.

Jackson pulled on an old ratty t-shirt that he'd thrown haphazardly on the chair in the corner and his briefs, and watched unapologetically as Alexis covered up his magnificent body.

"I think you're really going to like Austin," Jackson said, as they walked into the living room to wait for his ride share to show up.

Alexis' mouth quirked up into a smile. "Even though you hate Texas?"

"I don't *hate* Texas," Jackson said, even though he kind of did. Felt it even more strongly now, since the state was taking such a great guy away from him. *The perfect guy for you*, Jackson thought, and then blocked that particular thought out too. He didn't need to make this any worse than it already was.

"Well," Alexis said, "maybe if you don't, and you ever find yourself there, you can look me up."

Jackson nodded, even though he knew he never would. *Alexis* probably knew that he never would, but it was a sweet thing to say, anyway. In fact, it was a very Alexis-like thing to say.

Alexis' phone dinged, and a pair of headlights pulled into view, parking in front of Jackson's bungalow. "I think my car is here," he said, sounding very regretful. "I'm sorry to have to leave you this way."

"Me too," Jackson whispered, the pain arcing inside of him. "Safe travels."

"Take care of yourself," Alexis said. "Don't work too hard."

"I could say the same for you," Jackson countered. His fingers gripped the edge of the couch. He wanted *so badly* to tell Alexis to stay—but he knew that the word choice alone made it obvious that he shouldn't. He didn't want to *ask*. He wanted to *tell*. And how was that a good start to a relationship? It wasn't, and deep down, he knew it.

"One last thing," Alexis whispered, and caught Jackson's face in his palms, cradling him like he was the most precious thing in the world.

One last kiss, Jackson thought, and then all coherent brain function disappeared as Alexis' warm lips covered his.

It was a kiss that was somehow everything at once. A hello. A goodbye. A whole relationship of ups and downs and happiness and sadness and the absolute blinding joy of falling in love and the despair of falling out of it, all in one moment. The fire of too many nights staying up late exploring each other's bodies. The warmth of sleepy mornings when they cuddled in bed and refused to let go of each other. It was everything, and it was nothing, and then it was over.

Alexis lifted his head. Jackson saw everything he felt reflected in his dark eyes. "I won't forget," Alexis said simply, and Jackson's throat froze.

He couldn't even speak, couldn't even say goodbye, as he watched Alexis straighten and then walk out of his house, forever.

Maybe it was better this way, Jackson thought, a horrible wave of disappointment cresting over him. He hadn't been certain he could actually *say* goodbye to Alexis, anyway. So he hadn't. Maybe that kept a bit of hope alive that they'd see each other again, when circumstances were different, and they weren't being separated by a cruel fate that didn't care that they'd only *just* found each other.

After a long moment, the car pulled away, headlights flashing in the living room as it turned around. Jackson stayed after it was gone though, hoping against hope that somehow Alexis felt the same tug he did, right in the center of his chest, right where he'd always imagined his heart was, and he'd, impossibly, stayed.

But he hadn't. He'd gotten in the car and left, and there was a part of Jackson that was glad it had been him who'd had to leave, because he wasn't sure he could've done it.

Finally, there was nothing to do but get up, walk into the kitchen where he spied the pan on the stove, the dishes in the sink, the candle still lit on the table, and he wanted, more than anything, to burst into tears.

But he didn't. He wouldn't let himself. He cleaned up, distracting himself with the soap and sponge, cleaning everything twice over, and wiping down not only the counters, but the stove, too.

Then, after turning off the rest of the lights and checking the lock on the front door, he went back to the bedroom. The sheets and quilt were mussed from their escapades earlier, and Jackson straightened them, considering lying down, trying to rest, because he was tired, but he already knew that sleep was going to evade him.

Instead, he took a hot shower, and then curled up on the chair in the corner, thinking of one thing and many things and nothing, all at once.

The one thought that seemed to override all others was the promise he'd made to himself, and to Alexis, that he would stop putting things off. That he would do the things he'd always wanted to do.

Tomorrow, he decided as his eyes finally flickered shut, he would start the list that would set the tone for the new year to come.

Chapter Seven

A WEEK LATER

"I really don't know what to do with you right now," Shaw said.

Jackson glanced up from where he was working at the bar, all the way off to one side. It was a Sunday night, so it was still busy and a little noisy, but he was also not cloistered off in his office either. It was one of the compromises he'd started making since New Year's Eve.

He'd also come in a few hours late today, because he'd met with one of the contractors he was getting a quote from this morning. He'd met with two others this week and was hoping to have finalized who he was going to be hiring to remodel his house in the next few days.

It had been hard since New Year's. He'd come in the day after, listless, with zero energy or drive, still feeling the effects of too much vodka and not enough Alexis, and had discovered a gift on his desk that had helped to wipe away at least *most* of his moping.

"Why?" Jackson asked as he finished reconciling yesterday's sales. "I thought you'd be happy. I'm living more, aren't I?"

"Yeah," Shaw agreed, wiping the bar with a towel. "And that's a good thing. I'm never going to argue about you being more present here and also being more present in your own life. But you're also existing in this weird forced cheerful state, like if you tell yourself enough times that you're okay, you'll be okay."

"I am okay," Jackson said, and then made a face, because even he could hear it. Worse, he could *feel* it. He knew Shaw was right, but he also didn't want to talk about it, because there was no point. He did wonder if Alexis had left Los Angeles after dropping by the Funky Cup one last time, gifting Jackson with the thing he hadn't quite figured out what to do with yet. But then, he'd overheard Tony mentioning his name on a phone call the other night, so chances were . . . he was still around.

Still an almost irresistible temptation. And one that Jackson knew he had to resist.

"Yeah, no. You're not." Shaw didn't seem to be pulling his punches today. "What if I told you that Alexis was still around?"

Jackson's heart leapt, and he tried to force it back down, tried to extinguish the burst of hope he felt. "But he's not *sticking* around. We both know . . ." He took a deep breath. "It'd be a bad idea to spend more time together."

"Why?" Shaw looked confused. "Because you like each other so much? That's the *whole damn point*."

"No," Jackson said, trying to stay patient. "Because we like each other *too* much, and when he leaves? God, it's going to be a killer. Worse even than it is right now."

"Maybe he wouldn't leave," Shaw said. "You could always ask him to stay." Like Jackson had not considered this possibility a hundred times. A *thousand*.

"Yeah, you know I can't do that," Jackson said. Regretfully. And that really did seem to be the buzzword of the New Year, didn't it?

"I'd love to hear why," Shaw said, intently. "Because it seems like total horseshit to me. Did the guy leave you his famous, never-to-be-shared hummus recipe or not?"

"Shhh," Jackson hissed. "Nobody knows about that."

"Except you, and me, and Alexis."

"He did it because . . ." Jackson trailed off. He still wasn't entirely certain why Alexis had left it for him, scribbled on one of the bar napkins. And at the bottom was a sentence he'd underlined twice, *And don't forget to peel the chickpeas.*

Jackson hadn't made the recipe yet, but he already knew it would taste exactly like Alexis' hummus, and truthfully, he couldn't quite bear that yet. So instead, he'd kept it in his top desk drawer, wondering if he should share it with his kitchen, and profit on the night they'd spent together—he didn't think Alexis would even be angry if he did—or if he should save it for himself, and think of Alexis every time he made it.

"He did it because he likes you," Shaw said, somewhat impatiently.

"Sometimes things don't work out," Jackson said, and he heard that annoyingly fake note in his voice again. He was so tired of saying it. So tired of *listening* to himself say it.

"Right," Shaw said, but he looked unconvinced. Thankfully, his attention was stolen by a group approaching the bar, looking thirsty, so Jackson was off the hook, at least for now. He wasn't stupid enough to believe that Shaw would let it go, but . . . maybe he wouldn't have to talk about it for the next twenty-four hours, and maybe in the next twenty-four hours, it would stop hurting so much. But he'd thought that every single day since New Year's and it hadn't happened so far.

The dinner reminder on his phone beeped. Another change he'd made after New Year's—forcing himself to stop work at a mostly civilized hour, and enjoy, with his brother and their friends, the haven he'd helped create.

He closed up his laptop and after stowing it in his office decided, after feeling his stomach rumble, that he might as well go check which food truck was outside that night. It might be Tate's truck, Say Cheese, and he loved Tate's grilled cheese.

Pushing the door open, he froze in his tracks.

It was impossible to miss the shiny blue and white truck, or Alexis' smiling face in the window.

Jackson opened his mouth, shut it again, and nearly went back into the bar, but it would be weird if he did that. He knew it would be weird, and he nearly did it anyway, because he didn't know how to *look* at Alexis and not want to kiss him more than he wanted to take his next breath.

Finally, he stumbled towards the truck, cursing his inability to focus, even though he *knew* he had looked at the food truck schedule just yesterday and had noted that Alexis was no longer booked any evenings outside the bar. He'd thought he was safe.

Except he was very much *not* safe.

"Hey," he said to Alexis, feeling like a very awkward teenager with a very obvious crush. "I didn't know . . ." He took a deep breath. "I didn't realize you were going to be here tonight."

Alexis' smile widened. "I know you didn't," he said.

"What? You knew?" Jackson wasn't sure what to think.

"Just a moment," Alexis said, and then shut the window, making a few people behind Jackson, likely customers who had been looking forward to the best hummus of their lives, grumble with annoyance.

He emerged out of the side door and gave a reluctant shrug to the muttering customers. "Sorry," he said, "I'll be back in a few minutes. Break time."

Jackson really didn't *want* Alexis to take a break to talk to him. Any additional contact and this was going to be so much harder than it already was. That was what they'd agreed on, right? Well, not *agreed* on, but it had been unspoken. Alexis had practically said it when he'd said it would be too hard if he spent the night.

"I'm so glad you came out," Alexis said, tugging Jackson over to one of the picnic tables they'd set out in front of the bar area. "Though I was willing to go into the bar to get you."

"To get me?" Jackson raised an eyebrow. "I wasn't aware . . ."

"No, you weren't." Alexis was smiling now, clearly amused as they sat down.

"I'm just not sure what's happening," Jackson said. "I thought we had an agreement."

"I didn't know how to tell you," Alexis said. "You . . . I did not expect *you* to happen. I did not expect to want there to be an *us*, but there can't be unless I stay here."

Jackson took a deep breath. "I wanted to ask you to stay, but I . . . I didn't feel right doing it. You need to make the right choice for your business."

Alexis raised an eyebrow as he caught both of Jackson's hands in his. "And what about me? What about what makes me happy that isn't the business? We talked about both trying to do more to make ourselves happy this year."

"I am, I am trying," Jackson said. He almost tugged his hands back. Why was Alexis making this harder than it needed to be? All he'd wanted was to find something to eat for dinner, and instead . . . they were going to hash this out anyway, despite all his attempts to avoid unnecessary pain. "I've set timers to make myself stop working. I was going to get dinner tonight, and I was even working *at* the bar, instead of hiding away in my office."

"I know," Alexis said, still smiling. Like he knew something that Jackson didn't. "I did something today, too. I made a big decision, and I convinced Tate to give me his date, because I wanted to tell you in person but well . . ." He hesitated. "I was afraid. Afraid you didn't care about me the way I cared about you. But then you walked outside, and I saw your face and I knew, I *knew*, you were feeling the same way I was."

"I've been miserable all week," Jackson confessed, squeezing Alexis' hands. Letting his eyes really *look* for the first time. Drinking in the sight of him, hair rumpled, blue t-shirt with white apron, eyes a little tired.

A little uncertain too, if Jackson thought he was reading them correctly.

"When I told you I didn't want to spend the night, it was because I liked you so much, and I didn't . . . I was thinking about doing something drastic and I thought, I should try to make this decision on my own, with a clear head." Alexis shrugged helplessly. "But it was impossible. It wasn't just you, it was everything you've done for this community. You gave Tony a place to connect with other food truck owners, and then they became friends, and now they're going to be partners. *You* did that, you and Shaw. And then I met you, and just . . . *wow*." Alexis' eyes crinkled as he smiled. "You bowled me over. From the first moment. I wanted so many things, and I didn't know how to get them, and then suddenly, it occurred to me, when I was sitting there, in your kitchen, eating the omelet and wanting this all the time, that I could *have* it. There was nothing forcing me to go to Austin. I could stay, if I wanted to, and I realized . . . I wanted to."

Jackson was floored. Flattered and shocked and speechless. "You . . . you want to? Does that mean you're not leaving?"

"Yes," Alexis said. "And if you don't want to date, or see each other again, I'd understand but . . . I really hope that next year, you'll not only spend New Year's Eve with me but New Year's Day, too."

"Yes, yes, *yes*," Jackson said, and he reached for Alexis, their lips meeting like they had so many times in his mind, over the last week, but this time the man he was so crazy about was real, and he was here, and most importantly, he wasn't going anywhere.

EPILOGUE

THE FIRST TIME HE'D ever seen Jackson Finley, he'd been walking out of the Funky Cup's front door, and he'd been clearly exhausted, gray circles under his dark eyes, lines creasing his forehead, and shoulders stooped, like he was carrying a world of burdens on his shoulders.

Alexis' first impression had been that Jackson was a guy who needed help, but who didn't want to accept it. But he'd thought at the time that maybe . . . maybe he would accept something that wasn't explicitly help.

And Alexis had known, deep down, that he'd never wanted to feed another man the way he wanted to feed Jackson Finley.

It had been the most obvious thing in the world to fill him a plate and refuse to accept payment.

He didn't even know the guy—even though he *wanted* to—and there wasn't much he could actually do to make his life a little easier. But he *could* feed him when he was hungry.

Had Alexis been more than a little disappointed that they'd only exchanged a handful of words before he'd escaped with the plate? Yes, but he'd told himself that it was okay.

He was leaving in a few weeks anyway, heading to Austin to start his new life. No matter how much Tony kept haranguing him about staying in LA, he'd only ever planned for this to be a stopping point, not the final destination.

Still, he hadn't expected what he'd found in Los Angeles.

Tony had told him that they'd built a great food truck community—a great *queer* food truck community—and he knew Tony's habit of exaggeration from when they'd worked together briefly in Portland, so while he hadn't completely discounted it, he hadn't been expecting anything like what he'd discovered.

The group that tended to gather at the Funky Cup were cool and talented and welcoming and there was not even a whiff of even *friendly* competition.

Everyone just plain loved each other, and treated anybody into their midst like they'd always been there. Even Alexis, who was only planning on being there a few months, found himself moving into Tony's brother-in-law's guest cottage, and discovered that Shaw Finley, who managed the food truck schedule at the Funky Cup, was thrilled to find him spots on it.

Truthfully, before he ever saw Jackson Finley, he'd had more than one stray thought of *what if I stay*. And then he saw Jackson, and then he *met* Jackson on New Year's Eve, and the thoughts became an avalanche.

Jackson was wry and sweet and he'd worked his ass off to create a safe space. He was also really, *really*, cute and Alexis had barely even tried to resist kissing him the first time, despite that he knew it was a mistake to make this even more than it was.

What it was became very clear, very fast: this was a one-night stand, even though they might want it to be something more.

But Alexis, who wanted so much more than he could justify taking, had realized that he couldn't let Jackson be a major part of his decision.

When he'd left Jackson's house after the best sex and the best post-sex omelet he'd ever had the luck to share, with the best guy he'd ever met, he'd known he needed to try to make an objective choice.

Would it be better for his business if he stayed here? Or if he went on to Austin, like he'd planned?

The abject misery that he'd faced the first morning into that decision period had been the first piece of evidence that making an objective decision would be impossible. Wouldn't anyone decide *anything* just to make this burning regret stop?

The second one was, of course, Tony.

Because Tony was Tony, he'd tried to interfere.

All in the goal of helping, of course.

On the way home from Jackson's house, Alexis had sent Tony a text, asking to further discuss the proposal that he'd been teasing him with. He'd known Tony was putting together a food truck collective of his own—he'd bragged about it enough—but he'd wanted to see the nitty-gritty details. He'd wanted to know what he was trading, by giving up the Austin gig, and maybe what he might be gaining.

Of course the first thing out of Tony's mouth was, "I saw you last night," followed by a wink that was so ridiculously over-the-top that Alexis could only laugh.

"Oh, you did? Well, guess what," Alexis said, "I saw you too!"

"I mean, I saw you with *Jackson*," Tony said under his breath as they sat outside one of the coffee shops that Alexis had discovered Tony liked to frequent. Apparently it was right by the gym where Lucas, Tony's boyfriend, worked out. Working out, Alexis knew, was not something that Tony typically did.

Thus why Tony was here, in the coffee shop, and Lucas was probably a few blocks away, slaving away at the gym.

"Yeah, we were together," Alexis said. But he hadn't come here to talk about Jackson. He was trying to *forget* Jackson. Even though he had already begun to assume that was a fool's errand.

"Together?" Tony's eyebrows shot up. "Oh, so he *did* try to convince you." Then they waggled, totally destroying any credibility Tony might have. "With his body, huh?"

Alexis rolled his eyes. "I want to talk about the food truck lot you're putting together."

"Yeah, of course you do," Tony said, "because Jackson convinced you with his *body*. I owe that guy drinks for the next thousand years."

"Hard to owe the guy drinks when he owns the bar," Alexis said.

"See, this is why you have to stay," Tony said. "You've got the right attitude. That's what we're looking for."

"What else are you looking for?" What Alexis really wanted to know was: did they have a plan? Did they have a location? Had they signed a lease? What was the overall plan for the space? What were the requirements? Tony was a lot of big talk, but he'd never been what Alexis would consider to be a good businessman. But that had been a few years back, and the Tony he'd known and the Tony who sat in front of him now, might have the same sarcastic, charming personality, but that was where the similarities stopped.

The Tony he'd known in Portland would never have gotten serious with a guy like Lucas.

Tony whipped a folder out of his lap while Alexis was sipping his coffee and he nearly choked on it as the guy spread out a printed business plan—*Tony* with a business plan, it was hard to even wrap his head around that—and begin to talk about it in detail that made Alexis do a major double take.

Almost every question he had was answered in Tony's first overview of the plan. Maybe this wasn't the Austin collective, but Tony wanted to build something special and important here in LA. And Alexis was beginning to think that he might want in on the ground floor.

"And," Tony finished with a flourish, "there's the added bonus of getting to stick around Los Angeles. And keep sticking it in Jackson Finley."

Alexis would be lying if he said that wouldn't be an *extremely* nice side benefit.

"I'm . . ." Alexis hesitated. "I'm trying to make the decision without taking Jackson into it."

"Really?" Tony looked a bit flabbergasted. "But you guys were . . . I don't know . . . *all* over each other. You made Lucas and me look cold-blooded, and I promise that doesn't happen all that often."

Alexis had made a habit of hanging out with Tony during the last few months, and he knew that was true. That was the only explanation he had for the way he flushed at Tony's words.

"I like him, I really do," Alexis said. "But I've got to make the best decision for my business."

"What about you?" Tony asked, like this was the most obvious question in the world.

"What about me?"

It was Tony's turn to roll his eyes. "Listen," he said, "I get it. You're a small-business owner. Being one myself I know how it can overwhelm you sometimes, until you don't always know where you begin and the business ends. But they *are* separate. And sometimes you've got to think about *you* and what *you* want."

"I . . ." Alexis didn't know what to say to that. It had been just him, the whole truck revolving around him and his recipes and his hard work for so long that Tony was right. He didn't really know where one began and the other left off. Kind of like Jackson and how he'd let the management of the Funky Cup overwhelm his own life.

He also remembered, very distinctly, how Jackson had talked about how he wanted to change. How he'd recognized that the way he was living wasn't healthy.

From the way Tony was hinting, it wasn't just Jackson who needed to change how he was approaching things.

Here was the thing—Alexis *knew* he was good. And not just good at making Jackson Finley scream, either. He knew how goddamn good his food was. He would be plenty successful here. Maybe not as successful as he might be in Austin. But what was he giving up in exchange for that success?

Alexis was suddenly very, very sure that he didn't want to find out.

"I'm actually surprised at how good this all looks," Alexis finally said. "You've impressed me."

"Yeah," Tony said. "I know you think I'm kind of silly. Frankly, I *am* kind of silly. But I know I can do this. And Ryan's a brilliant guy. You've met him a few times now, I know you've seen how smart he is."

Alexis had. He hadn't realized that Ryan was the financial backer for the lot. And that, *that*, changed things too. How many people would come to this food truck lot, knowing that Los Angeles Dodgers' star shortstop co-owned it?

A fucking ton. People here loved their sports.

"I have," Alexis said. Took a deep breath. "Count me in."

Tony's eyes grew very big. "You're sticking around?"

"I'm sticking around," Alexis said firmly. And it felt like the best decision he'd ever made.

Just now how to tell Jackson that he was, without making him feel like he was obligated to continue seeing him. They'd agreed on a one-night thing. There'd been no promises exchanged, and Alexis discovered now that he wished they had.

He might feel a little less like he was climbing out on a limb, not sure if he'd end up alone, or if Jackson would join him.

Watching Jackson come out of the bar reminded Alexis so much of what he'd felt the first time he'd ever seen him—except that now, the feelings flooding him were so much *more*.

Shaw had mentioned that Jackson was taking more time off from the bar, and setting timers so he wouldn't forget to eat dinner. While Alexis liked that idea in theory, he hated it in reality because that meant other guys, guys that were not *him*, were feeding his Jackson.

Maybe he'd only been lucky enough to do it twice—once, on the night they'd first met, and then again, after the most magical New Year's, when they'd sat across from each other, sharing an omelet, and he'd been desperate not to word vomit everywhere about how much he wanted to stay.

He'd known then that he couldn't just make this decision because he wanted Jackson in his life. But then, had he taken too much time to think about it?

The way Jackson's face looked strained tonight, despite the lack of dark circles under his eyes, made Alexis worried that he'd waited too long to figure this out.

But from the way Jackson's eyes lit up the moment they met his own, he *knew*. The way he knew that a tomato was going to be juicy and delicious. Or a piece of chicken would melt in your mouth after he grilled it. Or that one more clove of garlic in a batch of hummus would be way too much. He just *knew*.

And when Jackson told him *yes*, not just once, but three times, and then reached for him, kissing him like they weren't sitting outside his bar, but were instead in his house, in his bedroom, he knew even more.

It was undeniable now. He'd almost screwed everything up, but now he knew for sure: what he'd shared with Jackson hadn't just been for one night, it was going to be bigger and better and *longer.* This wasn't just a one-night stand, this was the beginning of something special.

Of course, just because Alexis knew it was special, didn't *also* mean it wouldn't be hard, sometimes.

Like when he came home to the little bungalow they were now sharing after a long day of work and instead of being able to relax, he discovered that everything was covered in drywall dust. Or when the painters woke him up at six in the morning. Or when Jackson broke his promises and worked late, after all. When *he* broke his promises and didn't take on another employee right away like he'd told Jackson that he would.

But, six months later, the house was nearly done, they'd made it through all the hard, difficult patches that inevitably happened in a new relationship. And even more wonderfully, Jackson's eyes still lit up whenever he showed up at the bar. Maybe because he was usually bearing gifts of the edible variety, but mostly because, Alexis liked to assume, Jackson was happy to see his boyfriend.

The word still sent a thrill through him.

He'd almost given this up by not staying.

It had been an insanely hot day, preceded by an insanely hot week—though Jackson liked to tell him that even though southern California was experiencing a stronger-than-normal heat wave, it was still cooler here than it was in Austin—and Alexis was tired of sweating.

Something he wasn't tired of was watching Jackson work.

With the onset of summer, he'd added a smaller bar to the back patio of the Funky Cup, because the heat made everyone thirstier than normal. And even though Shaw normally manned the bar inside the Funky Cup, Jackson had started taking over out here more frequently.

Alexis had grabbed a late dinner for him, but when Jackson hadn't shown up in the air-conditioned interior of the bar on time, he'd ventured outside, expecting to find his boyfriend exactly where he did: helping a line of people three deep at the outdoor bar.

He watched as Jackson made margaritas and poured shots and flicked the lids off beer bottles, all with an expert competency that probably shouldn't have turned him on as much as it did.

"I was going to ask what happened to you, but it wasn't very hard to figure out."

Jackson looked up and grinned widely.

"You missed your dinner alarm," Alexis said, walking behind the makeshift bar and dropping a kiss onto Jackson's upturned lips. "So I thought I'd bring you something to eat."

"You are my favorite person," Jackson said with an expression of awe and wonder that in the last six months had never gotten routine or old. Alexis was beginning to wonder if it ever would. "Can I get you anything?"

"Vodka?" Alexis asked, but smiled when he saw that Jackson already had the bottle in his hand.

Jackson slid the glass across the bar and Alexis felt everything inside him go soft and mushy. He just really loved this guy. And not just because of the free vodka. "Thanks, babe," he said, and gestured towards the bag he'd brought with his other hand. "Now, *eat*."

Alexis could see Jackson's hesitation. Could practically read the concern running through his mind.

"What if . . ." he started to say, but Alexis cut him off.

"Eat," Alexis repeated. "I'll deal with the bar."

"You're not licensed," Jackson said, which he'd pointed out about a hundred times at this point. Alexis had briefly considered actually *becoming* licensed so that Jackson couldn't use that as an excuse anymore. But it wasn't like that excuse had ever kept him from turning the bar over to Alexis anyway, and he did this time too, scooting over so Alexis could join him.

"I'm sure they're gonna come arrest me," Alexis teased him, loving how Jackson's cheeks went from flushed with the heat to flushed with something else.

He watched as Jackson grabbed himself a beer and then opened the bag he'd brought, squealing that he'd saved a handful of *dolmas* for him. They were not only Jackson's favorite—they were Los Angeles' favorite. He had tried keeping up with the demand, but had finally given up on that, and now people raced to try to make it to his truck so they could get some before he sold out for the day.

"Of course," Alexis said. He'd remove an organ if it would make Jackson smile that way. And he'd felt that way from almost the first moment they'd met. That alone should have told him that he would never actually be able to leave LA.

A couple approached the bar, and he dealt with their order as Jackson munched away next to him, making all the happy appreciative noises that Alexis had come to associate with him really enjoying his food.

"Good?" Alexis asked as he watched him devour a whole pita in about thirty seconds, all dipped into his famous hummus.

The only other person besides Alexis who had that recipe was Jackson, and he'd never done a thing with it. As far as Alexis knew, it was still tucked away in a drawer of Jackson's desk at the bar. If Tony had ever found out that he had the recipe, he'd never heard a peep about it. Which meant that Tony *didn't* know.

And that filled Alexis with another wave of love. Jackson was the first guy he'd ever met who loved *him*, not his recipes and not his food and not his heritage. Not even his looks, but the man underneath.

"Do you have some kind of feeding Jackson kink?" his boyfriend wondered as he started in on the second pita.

"Hmmmm?" Alexis wasn't a saint. Now he was inevitably thinking about feeding Jackson something else entirely. Maybe in his private office, with its handy couch.

"You're always trying to feed me," Jackson said, not sounding dismayed at all by that particular fact.

Alexis reached out and cupped Jackson's cheek. "I want to take care of you, always. I just wish I could be here every night." Some moments, he'd discovered, were right for the kind of dirty fucking that heated his blood and some moments were for sweet words that warmed his heart.

"I know," Jackson said, his dark gaze intense. Understanding. Alexis wrapped an arm around his waist and tugged him closer. Not giving a shit who saw them. Definitely sure that Jackson didn't either.

"I just . . ." The sweet words didn't always come so well to him, but he was trying, and sometimes, that was what mattered. "I just love you a lot, and that's how I show it."

"So it *is* a kink, then," Jackson teased, sounding very, very pleased. "I like it."

"I think you love it," Alexis pointed out.

"I do. I love *you*," Jackson said. It never got old, hearing those words.

They stood there for a long moment. Alexis wished they were already home, despite that he knew Jackson had hours left before he could close up.

Then he remembered something that had annoyed him this morning.

"Does that mean you finally called that painter back?" Alexis had to ask. He'd been dealing with the half-finished interior as long as he could. It was *time* for Jackson to prioritize dealing with the last of the remodel.

"No, but I will. Tomorrow morning," he promised.

More thirsty patrons approached, and Alexis dealt with them as quickly as he could, grabbing beers and pouring a vodka and soda.

When he turned back to Jackson, he'd just about finished the half a pita that he'd included with the rest of Jackson's dinner. He'd eaten the other half before locking up his truck, and he knew just how good it was.

Jackson's admiring gaze told him that he'd enjoyed it just as much.

"Hey," Jackson said, "I'm gonna run inside and see if I can get one of the other bartenders to cover for me for a few minutes."

"I thought you'd already finished eating," Alexis said slowly, not sure he was quite following—but hoping that Alexis was on the same page as him.

Maybe they could only steal fifteen minutes in Jackson's office, but he needed to be alone with him. They'd barely seen each other all week. And sex? Yeah, that definitely hadn't happened. Maybe Alexis had gotten used to celibacy before Jackson, but now he didn't just want him, he *needed* him.

"I did," Jackson said slyly as he slipped out from behind the bar. "But it turns out I'm still hungry for something else."

"You're incorrigible," Alexis teased. Their eyes met over the bar and it was like that first night, all over again. Better, and bigger, even. Because now they weren't just thinking about the possibilities, but the *reality* of how fucking great their life together was. "We're finally going to christen your couch, huh?"

"Hell yes, we are," Jackson said, his tone breathless. He leaned over the bar. "Kiss me," he said.

Alexis didn't need another word of invitation. He leaned in, too, and pressed his lips to Jackson's. It was unbelievable that each and every kiss was better than the last, but somehow, impossibly, it was true. Even the sleepy pecks and the absent-minded brief touches right before they fell asleep and the sloppy, *shared way too much vodka,* kisses, and the deep, hot, make-out sessions they never had quite enough time to indulge in.

"Five minutes?" Alexis murmured against Jackson's mouth as he pulled back.

"Five minutes, and my entire life," Jackson said, unexpectedly causing the butterflies still swooping through Alexis' stomach to flutter wildly. He'd never thought he'd want to hear those words; he hadn't really thought a relationship was possible for him. But Jackson had made it possible. He'd done that just by existing and letting Alexis fall as madly in love with him as Jackson had fallen for him.

Alexis' heart raced as he waited the interminable five minutes he'd promised.

Four and a half minutes in, the new bartender showed up, shooting Alexis a bored look. "Boss said you wanted me out here?" he said, talking to Alexis like he actually worked here. Someday, when Alexis was less determined to get Jackson naked and orgasming, he would tell him that. Everyone already thought he worked here. He might as well *actually* work here?

"Yeah," Alexis said. "We just need you to cover for a little bit. Fifteen minutes, maybe? Or twenty?" He'd be lucky if he made it through twenty minutes with an eager Jackson and didn't come his brains out.

"Right," the new guy said, rolling his eyes. "Twenty minutes it is."

Alexis nodded and took off towards Jackson's office. The air-conditioning hit him like a blast to the face, and when he passed by the main bar, he saw Shaw, Jackson's brother, shooting him a knowing look.

Okay, so everyone knew they were going to go fuck in Jackson's office. That was okay, right? They were two completely, totally, head-over-heels-in-love, consenting adults. If they wanted to fuck in the privacy of Jackson's office, in the bar that he *owned*, that was totally their prerogative.

He pushed open the door to the office without knocking and nearly swallowed his tongue.

Jackson was already naked and on the couch, a tube of lube on the floor next to him, and two fingers buried deeply in his ass.

"Shut the door!" Jackson hissed, and Alexis realized that he was still standing there, jaw dropped, cock hardening so fast in his shorts that he felt dizzy with it. He shut the door, and thanked God that Jackson's office was off a little used corridor. Nobody else had seen Jackson like this—because nobody else was *ever* going to see Jackson like this.

Only him.

"I swear to God," Jackson said, squeezing his eyes shut as his fingers hit a particularly good spot, "I swear to God, you took way longer than five minutes."

Alexis pulled off his shirt, toed out of his Converse and unzipped his shorts, letting them fall to the ground, along with his boxer briefs. "I think everyone knows what we're doing," he murmured as he kneeled on the couch, smiling briefly as the springs squeaked at his added weight. "I hope you're alright with that."

"All I care about," Jackson said, his gaze boring intensely into Alexis', "is you get in me as fast as possible."

"You're way more ambitious than most people give you credit for," Alexis said, stroking a hand down Jackson's flank, feeling the skin quiver underneath his hands. His fingers reached up and closed around Jackson's dick, and he barely contained a moan as Alexis began working him up and down, in perfect concert to the thrusts of his fingers.

"Fuck, fuck," Jackson said, his own rhythm floundering as the pleasure began to overtake him. "Fuck, you gotta get in me." He pulled out his fingers and Alexis felt everything go hot and cold at once. He really *did* because otherwise he might just come on the spot.

Who knew that fucking in the bar they'd met in, six glorious months earlier, would be such a goddamn turn-on?

Alexis reached for the lube, and after slicking it up and down his cock, leaned down and kissed Jackson as he lined himself up. They'd left condoms behind a few months back and there was nothing he loved more than the hot, tight feel of Jackson around him as he slid home.

"You can't make a noise," Alexis said, right before Jackson wailed out, and not quite trusting him to keep quiet enough, covered his mouth with his own, kissing him deeply as he began to move inside of him.

Jackson grunted as he thrust harder and dug his fingernails into Alexis' back, urging him faster and faster and soon enough the couch was squeaking again, along with his movements, but neither of them cared because it felt too good to care.

Alexis felt like he was burning up from the inside out as he lost himself inside Jackson's heat, inside their kiss that spun on and on, and left him bursting with pleasure, both of the physical variety and the mental.

He'd never known what this felt like. Never understood why people would do anything to keep it. But right now, if anyone interrupted them, he'd probably lose his fucking mind.

The truth was, he felt like he was losing a little of his mind now, as Jackson reached down between their damp bodies, grasping his own cock and giving it a quick pull before he was clenching around him, sending Alexis hurtling into his own incredible orgasm.

He came back down slowly.

When he opened his eyes, Jackson was staring at him, love and care and longing written in every line and curve of his expression. "Fuck," he said, laughing a little. "That was amazing. I think we probably traumatized half the bar, but I think I don't really care."

"Me either," Alexis said, reaching up and cupping Jackson's cheek. "I really goddamn love you, okay? Today, tomorrow, probably a hundred years from now."

"It's been a good year, hasn't it?" Jackson mused. "And you just made it a little better, honestly."

"Anytime you ask me to, I'm here," Alexis said. He knew Jackson understood that he meant it, but would he ever understand the lengths that he'd go to make him happy? Maybe not. And maybe that was okay. Hopefully they could enjoy every bit of their happy ending and never worry about fighting for each other.

In Alexis' case, it hadn't even been a fight. All he'd had to do was surrender and he'd fallen so deeply in love that he wasn't sure he'd ever find his way out.

Knew he never wanted to.

"Then, let's go take a victory lap," Jackson said. "I say we've earned it."

Alexis raised an eyebrow.

"For waiting six months to fuck in my office. I know everyone assumed we would, that very first night."

"Even if we didn't, it was the best night of my life," Alexis said, and meant it.

"Mine too." Jackson pressed a hot, quick kiss to his lips. "New Year's Eve? Definitely my new favorite holiday."

"Why? You gonna meet some other tall, dark, handsome stranger?" Alexis teased as he pulled out, swiping a bunch of tissues from the box on Jackson's desk to help him clean up.

"Nope," Jackson said, his eyes shining. "Only you. Always you."

DRIVE ME CRAZY

FOOD TRUCK WARRIORS #1

To read more about the Food Truck Warriors, check out this excerpt from the first book of the series:

It was absolutely, without a doubt in Tony Blake's mind, a setup.

Now, he might not normally *mind* a setup, but there was no question this was his brother's doing, and instead of Tony being mildly intrigued, he was a little pissed off. Was it not enough for Wyatt to end up married to a *hot*, funny, professional baseball player while Tony got his heart smashed into a thousand tiny little shards? Admittedly, it was usually Tony who did the leaving, and maybe this time he deserved to find out how much being dumped sucked, but Wyatt taking pity on him by finding some random guy for Tony to settle for felt like a step too far.

"Tony," Wyatt said jovially, a touch too friendly even for him, which was the thousandth reason Tony needed to believe this was not only a setup, it was a *bad* setup, "meet Lucas."

At least he could give his brother credit for finding someone cute. Lucas smiled, the skin around his eyes crinkling. He was short, much shorter than either Wyatt or Tony, and had a clearly *very* athletic build. An athletic build, complete with pecs and abs and biceps and quads that Tony might've been interested in exploring further, if Wyatt hadn't been the one responsible for all this.

"Hi," Lucas said, extending his hand. "It's great to meet you, finally."

"It is?" Tony questioned. People usually liked meeting him. He knew he was attractive, that he'd been hot with the short buzzcut he'd had back when he'd first moved to LA, to help Wyatt start his food truck, *What a Catch*, and that he was even hotter now that his hair had finally grown out, nearly to his shoulders. He had great hair; if the food truck business failed, he could always go on Instagram and become a fucking hair model or something.

"Wyatt's told me a lot about you."

It could probably have been scripted by the Setup God, that's how fucking transparent it was.

"I'm sure he has." Tony crossed his arms over his chest, and glared, because he did not want anyone's fucking pity, okay? Nobody's leftovers, nobody's scraps, nobody's galling sympathy. He was *just fine*. He could be single, even though he hadn't been in many, many years, and yeah, maybe he'd done his share of moping around, when the breakup had happened, but it was his first broken heart! Didn't you deserve a little wallowing, a little pity party, when the man you thought was the love of your life casually dumped you and said, "someday you'll understand why we wouldn't have worked out"?

Yeah.

Tony thought of the dartboard he'd made of Brody's face, currently tacked up inside the little cottage he lived in, set back from the main house Wyatt and Ryan owned, and felt a tiny bit better. He'd landed a great hit last night, right smack on Brody's annoyingly perfect nose, the one he was convinced Brody had had fixed. Nobody had a nose that perfect in real life. *Nobody.*

It was a nose that could've launched a thousand ships, and it had fucking launched Tony from the tentative idea that he *might* like guys into the full-on, no-holds-barred realization that he was absolutely not straight. It had taken some time, but he'd finally landed on the right label. Not that figuring out who he really was had convinced Brody to stick around.

Asshole.

"Tony, why don't you tell Lucas a little more about the truck?" Wyatt said, his glee evident and really fucking annoying. There were a lot of times that Tony kinda hated his brother, but right now was pretty high up on the list.

"The truck?" Tony asked in disbelief. That's what Wyatt wanted them to talk about? *Geez, you suck at this,* Tony wanted to tell his little brother. *How did you ever get a guy like Ryan Flores when your game has this much epic suckitude?*

Lucas leaned against the edge of the sofa in Wyatt and Ryan's living room. "Your food truck?" He asked, his own nose crinkling adorably. Damnit, he was pretty cute. And even worse, he was exactly the kind of guy that Tony had always guessed he might like. Brody was nothing like Lucas, of course, he was tall with dark hair, and really dark, intense, penetrating eyes. There'd been more than once that he and Brody had been mistaken for brothers. Which, *gross*. But yeah, Lucas was definitely cute, and from the way he was eying Tony, the feeling was probably mutual.

What was even worse than a setup? A setup that fucking *worked*.

"That's what I invited him here to talk about," Wyatt said, his voice betraying a hint of frustration, as he called out from the kitchen where he was putting the final touches on dinner. "The food truck."

When Lucas With the Cute Nose left, Tony was going to have a real heart-to-heart with his brother on what you did during a setup. You didn't throw two people together and then *keep fucking talking*. You left. You kept your distance. You hoped, against all odds, magic and fireworks happened.

"Really?" Tony asked. "Well, okay. The truck is called *What a Catch*, and we serve, well, I guess . . .LA food? California casual? Tacos, the occasional burger, some fresh fish, we're most famous for our mahi mahi tacos, actually."

"Sounds pretty good," Lucas said, and he only sort of sounded like he meant it. Which tracked, Tony supposed. Because everyone knew that Lucas hadn't come here to talk about their food truck. He'd come here because Wyatt had given him an invitation into Tony's pants.

"Dinner's just about ready," Wyatt called out again, and added, "Ryan should be here soon. Dodgers had an early afternoon game."

"Have you met him before?" Tony asked, because if Wyatt was going to continually interfere, then he would at least take advantage of the subject change.

"Met who?" Lucas asked idly. From the way he'd not-so-subtly looked Tony up and down, he'd been pretty sure he was interested, but now he just sounded bored. Which was *fine*, and not at all insulting. *Nope.* Because Tony had been Not Interested first.

"Ryan Flores, Wyatt's husband," Tony said impatiently. "You know, the baseball player. The famous one." *The rich one*, Tony mentally tacked on. Maybe that was why Lucas had agreed to any of this in the first place, maybe he needed money. Maybe he really wanted to try to get to Ryan. Well, he was going to have to rethink that whole plan, because Ryan was pretty fucking devoted to his brother. And Tony was even more devoted to the pair of them. Nobody was going to take advantage of his brother's kindness and his brother-in-law's natural generosity, not while he was around.

Maybe Lucas stupidly assumed that because Wyatt and Ryan had money, that Tony had money too.

He managed a pretty decent salary from the truck, because Wyatt's connections and their bomb food kept them pretty solidly in the black, and he could even save a big chunk of it, because living in Wyatt and Ryan's ADA meant his living expenses, especially for LA, were crazy low. Still, he hadn't always been the poster child for responsible decisions, and while he had some money saved, it wasn't exactly a fortune. It wasn't enough to go along with a setup, that was for fucking sure.

Lucas gave him a weird look. "No?"

"Ah well, you will. He's . . ."

"Stupendous? Amazing? The game winning player of the century?" Ryan asked as he walked in, tossing his motorcycle helmet on the couch and giving Tony a quick hug, before turning to Lucas. "You must be Lucas."

They shook hands, and Lucas seemed as vaguely disinterested in Ryan as he did in Tony, so it couldn't be the money, and he sure wasn't a fame whore, because Tony had seen plenty of those before, hanging off Ryan like he was God's gift to the world.

"That was you, then, who hit the winning walk-off today. I caught the end of the game as I was finishing my workout," Lucas said offhandedly. And Tony wasn't really surprised—how could anyone be that noticeably ripped and *not* care about sports—but he'd clearly not been impressed by Ryan in-person. So that *wasn't* why he was here, after all.

"It was me," Ryan said with a face-splitting grin. "I'm going to go say hi to Wyatt, see where we're at with dinner."

As he walked into the kitchen, Tony rolled his eyes. "He means, he's going to go make out with my brother. We might eat . . .sometime this century."

"You're not cooking?" Lucas asked, and unlike Ryan and his walk-off hit that won the game, he actually sounded interested. Plain and simple, this guy was *weird*. Tony couldn't get a read on him at all.

Tony shrugged. "It's Wyatt's kitchen," he said, and then lowered his voice, "and sometimes my. . .*less than conventional methods* annoy him. He's all officially trained, you know?" He didn't mention that he'd had six months of culinary school under his belt before he'd dropped out. Of course, he'd barely gone to class in those six months, but still. Wyatt had not only graduated, he'd done so with honors, and then worked his way up to the highest echelon of restaurants, Bastian Aquino's Terroir.

"Unconventional?" Lucas sounded even more intrigued.

"I mean, I'm not formally trained. Not like Wyatt. He likes things . . .*just so.*"

"How does that work on the food truck, then?" Lucas asked. His grayish eyes had gone soft. Like he genuinely wondered how the two brothers got along when they worked in such close quarters with such different backgrounds.

"It didn't, at all, at first, but now we figure it out," Tony said. Then hesitated. "Do you want a beer? I'm gonna grab one, because like I said, we're gonna be waiting for dinner for a while."

Lucas smiled again, and it was even warmer than it'd been just a moment ago. "Sure."

"Any preference?" Tony asked, but Lucas shook his head.

"Whatever you're having is totally fine."

Tony went to the small fridge built into the bar at the far end of the room and grabbed two Coronas. "I'd go into the kitchen for lime," he said apologetically, flipping the caps off with an expert motion, "but . . .I've interrupted them way too many times already."

Lucas grinned as Tony handed him one of the bottles. "Really? And they're married? How long?"

"Not long, almost a year, maybe?" Tony grimaced. "But Ryan hitting that walk-off hit. . .it's like a fucking aphrodisiac to them."

"Must be weird living with all that . . ." Lucas waved around. "You know. Happily ever after shit."

Is it really shit? Tony wondered. *And if it's shit, why are you even here?*

Once upon a time, Tony might have agreed with Lucas, but that was before Brody, and before he'd known what it felt like to get his heart smashed. To watch the man he loved walk away and resume his life like Tony had never been part of it. Not only had it hurt like fucking hell, it had also made Tony resolved that someday, he'd have that again, and it wouldn't be with some ungrateful piece of shit who didn't really care about him. He'd have it with someone like Ryan, who gave a *thousand* shits, and who was loyal and true and wasn't going to just casually stab Wyatt in the back because he could.

He'd find a real partner, someone he could love, who loved him back.

Unfortunately, he was ninety-nine point nine percent sure that it was *not* going to be Lucas with the Great Nose and Ripped Arms.

Wyatt would be disappointed, but secretly, nobody was going to be more disappointed than Tony himself. It was impossible to live in such close quarters with, as Lucas would put it, *all that happily ever after shit,* and not crave it for himself.

"It has its moments," Tony said.

"Does Ryan come around the truck often?" Lucas asked, picking at the corner of the label on his beer.

"I don't know how much you know about baseball, but it's pretty fucking crazy, the schedule they keep," Tony said. "He's not around much during the season. Sometimes Wyatt travels with him, and then it's just me."

"You run the truck by yourself?" Lucas questioned, looking surprised.

"I don't usually book us much, if I'm going to be by myself. And sometimes I get a friend or two in town who gives me a hand," Tony said. Hoping, even though he knew Lucas was *not* The One, that he was maybe a tiny bit impressed at how Tony could handle a kitchen, even when it was a really busy kitchen. What he didn't mention was that one of the friends, Jeremy, had just texted him a few weeks before, telling him he was making the move from Napa to LA permanent. He could work more hours now, Jeremy had said. Was Tony interested in hiring him? Tony was pretty sure he was, but he needed Wyatt's approval first, because that was how they'd figured out how to run the food truck—they did it *together*.

"Ah," Lucas said. "Could use a permanent set of hands, then," he added. So casually that Tony almost missed it. But then Wyatt and Ryan emerged from the kitchen, only slightly disheveled, which meant that Tony might not have to totally disinfect every flat surface this time, and Wyatt said, "Tony's really going to need your help, Lucas, when I start working on the cookbook and also traveling this summer, with Ryan."

Everything shifted into sudden, painful clarity.

"What," Tony stated flatly. "You hired this guy?"

Wyatt shot his brother a lopsided grin. "Sort of? Let's call this . . .sort of an impromptu job interview? But yes, I'm hiring him. *We're* hiring him."

"I don't understand," Tony said. "This isn't a setup?"

Lucas shot him a slanted, knowing look. Maybe it could've still been, but of course Tony had just inserted his foot into his own mouth. Repeatedly.

"It's a job interview," Wyatt said sternly. "Geez, do you *ever* do anything but think about your cock?"

Begin the Food Truck Warriors by reading *Drive Me Crazy*, available on Amazon and Kindle Unlimited.

INTERESTED IN READING MORE OF
BETH'S BOOKS?

CHECK OUT A FULL LIST OF TILES
BY SCANNING THE QR CODE
OR VISITING HER WEBSITE

WWW.BETHBOLDEN.COM/BOOKLIST

WANT TO FOLLOW BETH?

MAKE SURE YOU NEVER
MISS A RELEASE?

SCAN THE QR CODE BELOW
OR VISIT HER WEBSITE
FOR A SOCIAL MEDIA LIST,
NEWSLETTER SIGNUP,
AND SO MUCH MORE!

WWW.BETHBOLDEN.COM/ABOUT

www.ingramcontent.com/pod-product-compliance
Lightning Source LLC
Chambersburg PA
CBHW070426310726
48977CB00003B/850